The Woman

While I slept, my heart was awake.
I dreamed my lover knocked at the door.

The Man

Let me come in, my darling, my sweetheart, my dove.
My head is wet with dew, and my hair is damp from
the mist.

Song of Songs 5:2
Good News Bible -Today's English Version

RECKLESS SURRENDER

ROCHELLE ALERS

Genesis Press, Inc.

Indigo

An imprint of Genesis Press, Inc.
Publishing Company

Genesis Press, Inc.
P.O. Box 101
Columbus, MS 39703

ISBN-13: 978-1-58571-345-5
ISBN-10: 1-58571-345-7
Manufactured in the United States of America

First Edition 1997
Second Edition 2009

Visit us at www.genesis-press.com or call at 1-888-Indigo-1

*Dedicated with love to
my mother, Minnie Liza McLeary–
thank you for the gifts of the spirit–*

and

*my daughter, Noemi Victoria Alers–
thank you for the joys of motherhood.*

CHAPTER 1

She could not resist him

His smile slipped away. The shaft of sunlight streaming into the room bathed Rina in gold. It reflected off her tawny golden skin, shimmering through the lacy pullover. It glinted off the lightened streaks in her hair, and it caught the brilliant lights in her luminous eyes.

"I must thank you for what you've done for me, Rina."

She was rooted to the spot, unable to move. His steady gaze bore into her with silent expectation and Rina knew what was going to happen before he reached for her.

Hypnotically, trancelike, she moved into his embrace.

Gently, deliberately, Cleve pulled her closer until their hearts melted into a strong, steady, measured beating. His mouth covered hers hungrily, exploring and drawing from Rina what she would've freely given if only he had asked.

Her lips parted under his as the heat from his mouth flared into hers, filling her entire being with Cleveland Whitney's raw maleness, His embrace, his kiss, was so different, so foreign that Rina felt herself drowning in the feel and scent of the man holding her to his heart.

"Thank you, sweetheart," he murmured hoarsely, placing tender kisses down the column of her slender neck. "Thank you, thank you, thank you," he whispered over and over.

Rina was sailing, floating high above reality. Nothing mattered except that she felt free, freer than at any other time in her life.

"I'm going to accept Mrs. Whitney's proposal," Rina Matthews said softly to the three other diners at the table. A myriad of expressions followed her announcement.

"Do you need someone to look after your apartment while you're away, sister?"

Gabriel Matthews ignored his son's request as he turned his attention to his daughter. "Have you thought this out, Rina?"

"Yes." The single word was emphatic. She had thought about the offer for nearly a week.

"Dad," Scott pleaded.

Gabriel shot Scott a warning glance. "You can talk to Rina about it later."

"Yes, sir," Scott conceded.

Rina laid aside her fork, staring at her brother, step-mother, then her father, offering each a smile. "It wasn't an easy decision to make, but the positives outweighed the negatives."

"But isn't it somewhat unorthodox to live with a client while auditing their books?" Evelyn Matthews questioned.

"It all depends on the client," Rina explained. "But if you're Abigail Whitney you can be as unorthodox as your resources permit you to be. She's offered us the account, but only on her terms."

"I wouldn't mind her terms," Scott commented. "I'd be willing to give up seeing Vicky Taylor just to spend the next two months waking up to the sight and sound of sand and pounding surf."

"I suppose that doesn't say very much about the girl you were ready to die for less than two days ago," Evelyn teased.

Color suffused Scott's tawny brown skin as he lowered his head in embarrassment. "Well, not quite," he admitted.

Rina enjoyed the weekly visit with her family. They always reminded her that there was a stable, saner side to life. Lately, it seemed as if events were happening faster than she could keep up with them. Eighteen months earlier she'd gone into partnership with a former class-mate, setting up a business management and accounting firm.

The first six months she and Jason picked up eight new accounts, then lost three of them without warning. They re-evaluated their strategy: Jason would handle marketing while Rina would concentrate on managing the office.

Harper and Matthews then courted bigger accounts, updated their computer system and hired an additional accounting clerk. Jason and Rina solidified their relationship in and out of the office. Everyone assumed that Rina and Jason would eventually merge their partnership by marrying.

She loved Jason, but she was not in love with him, and she still did not feel secure enough to marry him. Not yet. There was something missing in their relationship, and she hadn't discovered what it was.

"With you gone Jason is going to have to do some work for a change," Gabriel mumbled under his breath. "No more three hour power lunches for Mr. Smooth-Talker."

Rina knew her father disliked Jason, and he never bothered to hide it from her. Gabriel felt that Jason was too urbane, gregarious.

"There's no doubt that he'll have to spend more time in the office," she agreed, immediately defusing what always became an uncomfortable situation whenever she defended Jason.

"Your father's right," Evelyn stated. "We see you work yourself down to the bone while Jason has perfected his grin to where he should patent it."

Evelyn's comment surprised Rina. Never had her stepmother openly voiced her opinion of Jason. In the past she had always remained neutral.

Her hazel eyes shifted to her brother. "You may as well have your say too."

Seventeen-year-old Scott Matthews needed no prompting. "The brother may be many things, but a fool is not one of them. He knew he struck the mother lode when he hooked up with you."

"Amen," Gabriel said loudly.

There was a long, brittle silence. Rina had known of her father's dislike of her choice of a husband and business partner, but not Evelyn and Scott.

Anxiety spurted through her. Had her family voiced what she'd felt, been feeling for a long time? Her bright smile belied her sagging spirits.

"I suppose my spending the next two months at Mrs. Whitney's summer home near Sapelo will clear the air about a lot of things, won't it?"

"You'd better pray that it does, or you're going to be one sorry soul if you marry that boy," Gabriel replied.

She picked up her fork and concentrated on finishing what was left of her Sunday dinner. She didn't want to think that the people she loved most despised the man she had selected to spend the rest of her life with. She cut into a tender slice of lamb, a frown creasing her smooth forehead as she wondered what it was about Jason that kept her from a total commitment.

Rina was a realist, never indulging in fantasies. She had been that way since the age of eight when she watched her mother grow weaker and weaker even though her father and several doctors reassured her that Rebecca Matthews would survive the debilitating illness laying waste to her young body.

Rebecca Matthews died at twenty-eight, leaving a grief-stricken husband and brokenhearted daughter consoling each other. And when Rina sat on the window seat in her bedroom staring out the window she began planning for her own future. She wanted her own business, she wanted to travel, and she wanted to marry and have children. Now at twenty-nine she had accomplished the first two, but getting married and having children was still a part of her future.

"What about your apartment, Rina?" Scott asked, breaking into her thoughts. His large, clear brown eyes widened in excitement and anticipation.

She gave her younger brother a warm smile. "You can look after it for me only if you promise not to trash it."

"All right!" Scott said between clenched teeth. He was hard-pressed not to let out his excitement.

"I don't want any loud parties, cigarette burns on my rugs, beer stains on any of the chairs and sofa, drugs or orgies."

"Rina!" Scott gasped, his uneasy gaze shifting to his parents.

"One mishap and you're back here," Gabriel warned in a soft, no-nonsense tone.

"I don't know what the big hurry is to get away from home," Evelyn complained. "In another few months you'll be at Morehouse." She was not ready to let go of her son and only child.

Scott left his chair, circled the table and kissed his mother's cheek. "Practice, Mama. It won't hurt to get in a little practice."

Rina stared at Scott as he leaned over Evelyn's shoulder. "I'm going to leave the number where I'll be staying with my neighbor. One call from Mrs. Thompson and I'm back on the first thing smoking. Then you'll have to deal with me, little brother." She was twelve years older than Scott and eight inches shorter than his six-two frame, yet she still thought of him as her little brother.

"You must be getting old, Rina. You worry too much." Scott ducked when Rina sailed a rolled-up cloth napkin at him.

"Watch your mouth, son," Evelyn warned. "I'm only ten years older than Rina, and what does that make me?"

A slight smile played at the corners of Gabriel's full mouth. "And I'm at the big five-o. What am I, ancient?"

Scott whistled softly under his breath, backing out of the dining room. "Whoa. You guys sure can get hostile about nothing. All I said was old…" He turned and sprinted from the room as two of her cloth napkins were thrown at his retreating back.

Gabriel stood up, shaking his head, and Rina rose with him. "What are we going to do with him? I wonder when he's going to grow up."

Rina placed her palms against her father's solid chest. "He's growing up, Daddy. You don't see it because he's around all the time."

Gabriel's arms went around her slender shoulders. "And you're not around enough," he said in a gruff voice. "You work six days a week, and when you're not working you're out with Jason Harper. Evelyn and I never plan anything for Sundays because we don't want to miss having you for dinner."

Rising on tiptoe, Rina kissed her father's neatly-barbered bearded cheek. His short beard was salt and pepper gray while his hair held only a trace of silver.

"All of that is going to change soon, Daddy. After this summer I'm going to stop working so hard. The Whitney account will bring my company the revenue it'll need to stay solvent through our fiscal year."

Gabriel pressed his lips to Rina's curly hair. "I hope you're right, baby." Pulling her closer, he held Rina in a protective embrace. "I still can't believe you've grown up, Rina, and that you have a life of your own. You've made me proud, baby girl."

She wound her arms around Gabriel's neck. "And I love you, even if you do worry needlessly about me."

Evelyn slipped surreptitiously from the room, leaving Gabriel and Rina to share their private time together since her husband always complained that he didn't see his daughter as often as he wanted to. Yet, whenever Rina and Gabriel shut her out, Evelyn experienced spasms of jealousy about the dead woman who had been his first love.

Rina was an exact replica of Rebecca Matthews. She had inherited Rebecca's palomino-gold brown skin, expressive hazel eyes, full mouth and rich chestnut-brown, curly hair that lightened with streaks of gold in the hot summer sun.

"Speaking of babies, what do you say about bouncing a grandchild or two on your knee?" she asked Gabriel.

His fingers tightened on her body. "You're not expecting are you?" A flash of panic clouded his dark eyes.

Rina glanced up, shaking her head. "Of course not."

A muscle throbbed in her father's temple. "Now you know that if you ever need to talk to me about something, anything, I'm here for you."

She nodded. Somehow she failed to get her father to see that she was no longer eight but twenty-nine. Easing out of his embrace, she said, "You've always been here for me. Daddy."

Gabriel ran a hand over his face, then stared at Rina from under lowered lids. "Are you coming back at any time during the summer?"

"I'm going to try and get away at least once each month."

"Do you need help getting your things together for the trip?"

She turned away and began clearing the dinner table. "No thanks. I'm having all of my clothes and personal items shipped. I have just enough room in my car for myself and a briefcase."

Everyone had been surprised when she decided to buy the low-slung convertible two-seater. Her father teased her, saying he always expected an accountant to buy a practical-looking sedan, not a vehicle built for speed.

But it had been the one time she wasn't practical. She saw the Corvette in the dealer's showroom and fell in love with it. She called it a reckless impulse when she told the salesman she would be back the following day to pick it up.

"When are you leaving?" Gabriel questioned.

"Wednesday morning."

He let out his breath slowly, "Drive carefully, Rina."

She knew the cause of her father's anxiety. He did not handle separations well. Gabriel Matthews had never adjusted to losing his first wife.

"Of course, Daddy. I'll come by Tuesday night to say good-bye."

His expression brightened. "Good. Very good."

She carried the dishes to the kitchen and handed them to Evelyn who stacked dishes, glasses and pots in the dishwasher.

"Take care of my father, Evelyn."

Evelyn's hands stilled, and she turned and stared at her stepdaughter. "You know I will."

Rina held out her arms and Evelyn went into her embrace. "Thank you, Evelyn." She kissed her cheek. "Thank God he has you."

Evelyn's friendly dark eyes searched Rina's hazel ones. "It's not easy loving Gabe. I know he can't give me what he doesn't have, but I hope beyond hope that someday I'll get a little of what he gave your mother."

Rina examined the petite woman who was more a sister than a stepmother. "He loves you, Evelyn. He may not say it all the time, but he loves you very, very much."

Evelyn nodded, blinking back tears. "Maybe you're right."

"I know I'm right."

The two women cleaned the kitchen, then rejoined Gabriel in the dining room for coffee and generous slices of coconut cake.

She spent another hour talking and laughing with her family, then gathered a plate of food Evelyn had prepared and insisted she take home. Evelyn always complained that Rina didn't eat enough to keep a bird alive.

Dusk had descended and fireflies flitted lazily in the sultry Atlanta night when Rina slipped behind the wheel of her car for the return trip to her apartment several miles from the Georgia city's business district. A half hour later she parked in the driveway to her duplex condominium apartment.

She let herself in and stood in the entry looking at the sparse, but elegantly furnished, space. The walls, floors and furniture were a stark white. A splash of color from throw pillows and flowering plants broke up the sea of endless pristine alabaster. In only three days she would be leaving it. She had no doubt that Scott would water her plants and occasionally wipe away a layer of dust, and that her apartment would remain unaffected, but would she? Would two months away from Atlanta and Jason give her the time she needed to find out what was missing in their relationship? And because she loved Jason, she prayed it would.

CHAPTER 2

The sky was beginning to brighten with streaks of mauve, pearl, gray and bits of blue. The sun inched higher in the heavens as Rina began the three-hundred-mile drive from Atlanta to Sapelo at dawn. Pine, weeping willow, weeping beech and oak trees draped with Spanish moss stood along the side of the road like sentinels, keeping watch on everything and everyone who passed and admired their majestic summer dress.

She drove with the top down, savoring the smell and warmth of the Georgia air against her face. She loved and appreciated her home state. She loved its people, the beauty of its varying topography, its charming Southern aristocracy.

The Savannah Whitneys were Southern aristocrats. The Whitney name was synonymous with history, money and social elegance, and their business interests extended to banking, insurance, publishing and several radio stations.

And it was the Whitneys who had begun the age-old tradition of hosting Savannah's renowned black and white ball.

Southern Accents, a magazine of fine Southern homes and gardens, had devoted a cover story to Whitney Hall. The story reported that a Whitney had hosted the first black and white ball, not to humiliate the impoverished landed gentry after the Civil War but to celebrate a sizeable inheritance from a distant cousin who had been the mulatto son of a wealthy Louisiana Creole planter.

Noah Whitney invited all of Savannah's people of color to attend the festive soiree. The attendees wore unbleached cotton or muslin or the much evident black, which symbolized the loss of a loved one. Subsequent annual gatherings gained popularity for the privileged people of color who were fortunate enough to receive an invitation to attend the Whitneys' elegant black and white ball.

Rina had Jason to thank for securing the Whitney business accounts. Jason had attended a high school reunion, renewing his close association with Philip Whitney. With Philip's intervention, Jason Harper used his dynamic marketing skills to convince Philip's mother to contract the services of Harper and Matthews.

She smiled, remembering her first encounter with Jason Harper. Not many could resist Jason once he turned on his charm. Rina had not been exempt when she met the charismatic man in a graduate program at Georgia State University.

All thoughts of Jason and the Whitneys fled as Rina entered Macon's city limits. She ordered a full breakfast, lingering over it for almost an hour before resuming her trip southward, hoping to stop only to refuel the Corvette and stretch her legs.

The soaring, early June temperature forced her to put up the top of the convertible and turn on the air-conditioning. The lightweight cotton dress no longer clung to her moist flesh as she increased her speed. It was nearing the noon hour when the distinctive smell of the ocean filtered through the vents. She curbed the urge to stop in Savannah and continued south.

Oak trees gave way to palm trees and rolling lawns to streets littered with sand. The Whitney summer retreat was not situated on Sapelo Island, but Jason had informed her that the island could be seen from the windows on the upper floors of the historical structure.

She followed the detailed written landmarks and found herself following an unpaved road that seemed endless. Then, like a breath of wind or a flutter of an eyelid, it appeared before her, sparkling like spun confectionary sugar on dark green velvet. The blue-gray water of the Atlantic Ocean was the backdrop for the four-story white house with its octagon-shaped upper floors.

The feature article in *Southern Accents* had not begun to depict nor describe the exquisite beauty of the grand house that was framed by ancient cypress trees. Wing pavilions, a Greek Revival facade and a Regency-style entrance topped by an octagonal cupola gave the structure a wedding cake appearance.

So this is to be my home for the next two months, Rina thought. Scott was right. She, too, would be willing to give up Jason Harper's company for the verdant splendor of the Whitneys' summer residence.

The powerful engine of the Corvette purred softly in the quiet afternoon as she maneuvered into a circular brick-paved driveway. Cutting off the engine, Rina surveyed the other automobiles lining the opposite curve of the driveway. A stately black Mercedes classic sedan, an apple-red Porsche and a late-model silver-gray BMW coupe were all vying for equal attention.

The front door opened and a young woman who appeared to be in her mid-twenties skipped lightly down the steps. The sunlight caught the brilliance of a band of diamonds on her left hand and glinted off a crown of thick, black hair. The sweep of a sleek pageboy brushed against the white raw silk of a tailored blouse as she glanced over her shoulder.

"Thanks again, Cleve."

"Don't forget to call me, Maddie," returned a strong, mellow masculine voice.

The woman named Maddie touched her fingertips to her lips and blew a kiss at the tall man framed in the doorway. "I won't, darling."

The man cradled a child in his arms. His expression indicated a less than happy parting. "Don't force me to call you, Maddie."

Maddie halted her retreat, her hand staying at the door handle to the Porsche. "I said I'd call you and I will," she snapped angrily. Seconds later she backed out of the driveway with a squealing of tires.

Cleve's dark eyes narrowed, his gaze fixed on the flash of red until it disappeared from view. Only when Rina stepped out of her car and walked toward him did his rigid stance relax.

Rina wished she hadn't witnessed the tense domestic exchange and she chided herself for not stopping to brush her hair or smooth the wrinkles out of her cotton dress. Seeing the elegantly dressed Maddie reminded her that sitting in the confines of a car for more than six hours was not conducive to presenting an impeccable first impression.

She watched the tall man watch her as she drew closer. And for the first time she realized he was dressed all in white: short sleeve knit shirt, linen slacks and deck shoes.

His mahogany coloring was smooth and glowed with a rich, healthy sheen in contrast to his attire. He shifted the sleeping child, and a ripple of firm muscle flexed under the skin of his upper arm.

She could not ignore his perfectly honed body as she tilted her head to meet his fathomless dark eyes examining her moist face. A slight ocean breeze stirred wisps of sun-streaked curls that had escaped the single braid resting along her straight spine.

"I'm Rina…"

"I know who you are," Cleve interrupted. "My mother is expecting you."

Standing only inches from him, she suddenly realized who he was. Cleveland Whitney: brilliant, arrogant, wealthy, and one of Savannah's most sought-after
bachelors. Rina felt and recognized his resentment
immediately. Jason had informed her that Abigail
Whitney over-ruled Cleveland's recommendation that
she not change accounting firms.

"If that's the case, kindly inform Mrs. Whitney that
I've arrived," she ordered quietly.

An arching black eyebrow inched up slightly at her
authoritative retort as Cleve's gaze narrowed. Her
attention was fixed on his full lower lip. She thought
she detected a pout before his lips parted in a smile.
And it was his smile that melted away any hint of
annoyance she may have felt.

His smile was dazzling, blinding. Parted lips
displayed perfect white teeth. A slight overbite
enhanced his wide mouth rather than detracting from
it. Shifting the sleeping child against a muscled
shoulder, Cleve extended his right hand.

"I'm sorry," he apologized. "My sister Maddie is the
only person in the world who can rattle my cage
without even trying. Welcome to Whitney."

She took the proffered hand and smiled. "Thank
you, Mr. Whitney."

His fingers tightened briefly on hers before he
released them. "Cleve. Around here everyone's pretty
informal."

The little girl stirred restlessly. The thumb of her left hand found its way to her mouth. Lowering his chin, Cleve rested it on top of the child's head.

She noted the fine curly hair sticking to the child's damp forehead, then her sucking mouth. A fringe of delicate lashes lay on her flawless cheeks.

"She's quite beautiful."

"That she is," Cleve agreed. "This little lady is very special to all of us." There was more than a hint of pride in his voice.

Rina noticed a slight resemblance between man and child. The curve of the eyebrows, jaw and chin were similar.

"What's her name?"

"Emily-Jane Whitney Jackson."

Rina laughed softly. "That sounds like a mouthful for a little girl."

"She is a mouthful. The only time she isn't talking is when she's asleep." Cleve extended his hand again. "Please come into the house. My mother will read me the riot act for entertaining on the front porch."

She felt the warmth from his strong fingers curving around her bare upper arm. She stepped into the coolness of the entry beside Cleve and felt successful when she didn't gape at the magnificent curving stairway leading up to the fourth-floor octagon.

Cleve glanced down and met her entranced gaze. "I'll leave the house tour to Mother."

"It's somewhat overpowering," she admitted, feeling at ease for the first time since encountering the formidable Cleveland Whitney. Political rumors were circulating that this Savannah district attorney had challenged the incumbent mayor for his seat in the upcoming election.

"Oh, there you are, sweetheart. Poor little baby. You must be exhausted from that long trip," crooned a softly modulated feminine voice. "What are you doing, Cleveland Graham Whitney? Why are you just standing there with that child? Come, let me put her to bed."

A tall slender woman with short silver hair hadn't paused to inhale as the words tumbled from her lips. Cleve took a step and she saw Rina for the first time.

"Were you entertaining that girl on the front porch?"

Cleve leaned over, his hot, moist breath washing over Rina's ear and cheek. She shivered in spite of the heat. "What did I say about the front porch?" he whispered, again flashing his arresting smile.

Rina nodded conspiratorially. Moving away from Cleve, she crossed the highly-waxed pale oak flooring and presented herself to Abigail Whitney.

"After our telephone conversation, it is my pleasure to finally meet you, Mrs. Whitney."

Abigail placed both hands on Rina's shoulders and pressed her scented cheek to the younger woman's. "I must say it's my pleasure, Rina." Large, dark brown eyes swept appreciatively over Rina. "Looks and brains," she said softly. "A most winning combination."

"Thank you, Mrs. Whitney." She had grown used to compliments about her looks. As a child she remembered her mother's stunning beauty and had heard her family's comments on how much she resembled Rebecca.

"Please call me Abigail. You'll be living here for most of the summer, so try to think of yourself as family."

"Excuse me. Mother, Rina. I'm going to put Emily-Jane to bed," Cleve announced.

Abigail ran a slender hand through expertly coiffed hair. "I'll do that. Why don't you show Rina her room? After she's settled in, give her the tour so she'll know where everything is." She removed the sleeping Emily-Jane from her son's arms and walked out of the spacious living room.

Cleve's handsome features settled into the tight expression Rina remembered when first meeting him. Despite his easy smile, it was apparent Cleveland Whitney had not changed his mind about his mother retaining the services of Harper and Matthews to manage her personal and business holdings.

He stared at her, unblinking. He went still. Only a throbbing muscle in his lean jaw indicated Cleve was breathing, existing. This was the stance she had read and heard about. She was seeing for herself how the intimidating prosecutor successfully won every case he took on for the state.

Rina tilted her chin and gave him a steady look. At five-six she wasn't short, but having to look up at a six-foot, three-inch Cleveland Whitney put her at a disadvantage.

"I know you don't want me here," she began, deciding to attack first.

He blinked once. "You're right about that. But there's nothing I can do about it. It's my mother's finances you're controlling, not mine."

"The word is managing."

Cleve pushed his hands into the pockets of his slacks, and his breath came out in a long shudder. "The only difference between you and your slick partner is that you're a lot more beautiful than he is." He ignored her soft gasp. "I don't trust him, never did, and I don't trust you. If you and Harper are playing some sort of con game to steal my mother's money, I'll make certain the two of you spend so much time in prison that you'll forget your own names."

Rina shoved her own hands into the large pockets of her dress. Never had she wanted to slap anyone more than she did Cleveland Whitney at that moment. He was calling her a thief.

"You've warned me, but now let me warn you. I don't scare easily, Mr. Whitney. I haven't been accused of any crime, so you can drop the legal posturing…"

"It seems as if you're going to be a worthy opponent," he interrupted, apparently enjoying her challenge.

"I will not tolerate your interference," she shot back.

Cleve smiled again, this time looking more like a predator ready to pounce and ravish his prey. "I'm not going to interfere, Rina. But I'm going to be watching you and waiting for you to slip up. Hustlers usually do." He took a step closer, grinning down at her angry features. "I'm going to stick closer to you than stink on a pile of dung."

Pinpoints of brilliant green flashed in Rina's eyes as she struggled to control her temper, because she did not intend to trade another barb with the arrogant, suspicious man. She needed all her wits to do the best job she could for her client.

"Show me to my room, please," she demanded, her voice laced with annoyance and fatigue.

"This way," he said flatly.

Rina followed his lead up the curving staircase. She didn't know why, but she felt like a prisoner being led to jail. Why did she feel as if the most exciting career opportunity had suddenly become a sentence of hard labor? Why had Cleveland Whitney condemned her before she had a fair trial? What had Jason said or done to arouse the man's ire?

She would talk to Jason about his meeting with Cleve, but first she needed to shower and change her clothes. Hopefully after her conversation with Jason she would be able to clear the air with Cleve. He had called her a worthy opponent. What Cleveland Whitney did not know was just how worthy she could be.

CHAPTER 3

"Your clothes arrived yesterday," Cleve informed Rina as he opened the door of a room at the end of the hall on the second floor. He stepped aside and she walked into the bedroom. "Mother selected this room. I hope it'll be to your liking."

Her gaze took in everything in the large room. "It's quite charming."

And it was. The furnishings evoked the timeless and unpretentious beauty of the French. Pale wood with hand-painted floral designs graced a massive armoire, headboard, dresser and chest of drawers. A bouquet of dry herbs lay on the grate in the unlit fireplace instead of the usual stack of wood.

"I wouldn't want you to feel uncomfortable while you're here," Cleve continued, his voice registering genuine concern.

She sank down into the rocker and pressed her head against a yellow floral print cushion. She stared up at Cleve under lowered lids. "Thank you." She wanted to ask him if he actually cared whether she was comfortable or not, but didn't.

Cleve suddenly seemed aware of how tired she was. "Why don't you take your time settling in. I'll have

Mrs. Bailey keep something warm if you sleep through dinner."

Rina closed her eyes. "Thanks," she mumbled softly.

Cleve watched the sweep of her gold-tipped lashes on high cheekbones. His gaze moved slowly over a minute mole on her right cheek, then to a matching one over the rising swell of her right breast revealed by the V-neck bodice of her sundress. Streams of sun pouring through the lacy panels at the French doors bathed her in gold. Gold on gold.

He backed out of the room, closing the door. The bedroom Abigail Whitney had selected for Rina couldn't have been better if Cleve had selected it himself. Rina Matthews had stepped into a trap of her own choosing, and it was only a matter of time before Cleve sprang it.

Rina snuggled against the pillow, wrapping both arms around the fluffy mound of feathers covered by an embroidered pillowcase. Ribbons of wakefulness threaded through her head as she struggled to pull her mind and body out of a state of somnolence; however, sharp contractions in her stomach won out. She had to wake up and give her body the nourishment it demanded.

Opening her eyes, she was overcome by darkness and silence.

She sat up suddenly, remembering she wasn't in her own bed. She was at Whitney Hall.

Forcing her body off the bed, she walked across the bedroom to the set of French doors and opened them. She inhaled a lungful of salt-filled air. A canopy of black with a liberal sprinkling of stars and a slip of a moon was the only illumination in the nighttime sky.

The smooth wood planking of the veranda was cool to her bare feet as Rina moved over to the decorative wrought-iron railing. The sound of the Atlantic rustled, a gentle lapping in the stillness. She caught the faraway sound of a night bird and the incessant chirping of crickets. It was as if nature was giving her a private performance. The peace and solitude stole through her body, willing her to partake of its hypnotizing feast.

Thinking of a feast, she turned and went back into the bedroom, making her way to an adjoining bath. She pulled her nightgown over her head and stepped into a shower stall.

Thirty minutes later Rina descended the exquisite curving staircase with its hand-turned mahogany spindles. Soft light reflected from a massive rosette chandelier suspended from the ceiling. The soft swirls resembled icing on a decorated cake.

A babble of male and female voices drifted upward from a room off the living room, and it was apparent that the Whitneys were entertaining guests.

"Cleveland, please be a dear and freshen up my drink," crooned a woman's sultry voice.

His mellow reply was muffled by the incessant chatter and laughter, but Rina remembered just how soft it could be, even when he was verbally cutting her to pieces with his unjustified suspicions.

She had just reached the last step when a door opened and Cleve walked into the living room. His expression was one of surprise, then he recovered quickly. A slow smile crinkled his dark eyes as he stared at her.

She had changed into a pair of emerald green linen slacks and matching silk blouse. She had brushed her hair and pulled it back into a loose chignon at the nape of her neck. Her fingers went unconsciously to the small gold locket suspended from a delicate filigree chain around her neck.

"Good evening, Cleve." She did not register Cleve's reaction to her low, husky voice still laced with sleep, when he slipped his hands into the pockets of a pair of black slacks. He had also changed from his earlier white to all black: slacks, silk shirt and Italian-made loafers.

"Good evening, Rina," he returned. "You appear rested."

"I am, thank you."

Neither of them moved. It was as if their previous confrontation had never occurred.

She felt the power of his presence radiating through her. Tall, dark and dressed all in black, Cleveland Whitney was overwhelmingly virile and formidable.

He broke the spell when he removed a hand from his slacks pocket.

"I'd like you to meet some friends of mine."

Rina had come to Whitney Hall to work, not socialize. And certainly not with someone who thought she was a thief.

"Maybe some other time."

Cleve dropped his hand and walked over to her. He had a quick, light step for a large man. Each motion was fluid, graceful and quiet. He dwarfed Rina, enveloping her with the subtle fragrance of his cologne and body heat.

His gaze surveyed her smooth, shiny hair, dropping with agonizing slowness to the natural curve of her full mouth. "But everyone is anxious to meet my mother's beautiful house guest."

Rina was more annoyed than flattered by his statement. Cleve was baiting her.

"How can they be anxious to meet me when they know nothing of me?

He leaned closer. "They know all they need to know about you."

"You told them." It came out more like a statement than a question.

His lids lowered slightly over large, expressive eyes. "Yes."

"Did you tell them that I'm going to steal your mother's money?"

He had the grace to look uncomfortable. Turning away, Cleve glanced up at the chandelier. "No, Rina. I wouldn't insult you like that."

"You should've thought about that before you made me aware of your suspicions," she shot back angrily.

"How was I to react when my mother decided that the accounting firm who has been handling her finances for years is incompetent?" he countered. "Then I find out that she wants Jason Harper to manage her money. The same Jason Harper I've never liked, even if he was my brother's friend."

His gaze swung back to her, impaling her where she stood.

"Act three, enter Miss Rina Matthews who looked more like Harper's courtesan than his so-called partner."

Something inside of her exploded. "You sexist pig! Is that how you classify any female district attorney who walks into your masculine bastion? Do you conduct background investigations to see how many men she's slept with before she's admitted to your priv-ileged sanctum?"

Cleve's broad shoulders rose and fell heavily under his black silk shirt. "I'm sorry, Rina. I didn't mean it that way."

"You won't know what sorry is, Mr. Whitney," Rina continued recklessly, "unless you change your opinion of me. I didn't become a CPA to cheat people out of their money. But if I even suspect that you're spreading rumors about my not being honest, I'm going to slap you with a lawsuit charging you with defamation of character!"

His expression stilled and grew serious. "You wouldn't."

Rina felt a measure of satisfaction when she saw his stunned expression. "Try me," she said softly. "You're the one looking for votes, not me. Can your impeccable reputation withstand the negative publicity of an impending lawsuit?"

He crossed his arms over his chest, shaking his head. "I don't believe you would sue me."

"Just try me," she goaded.

His eyes flashed rage. There was a pregnant silence. "All right, you win. I won't interfere with you and your business dealings with my mother. You have my word on that," he added when she gave him a skeptical look.

She smiled. "Good."

First round: Matthews-one, Whitney-zero.

Rina basked in the knowledge of her power. She had temporarily bested one of the best.

"Now that we seem to have settled the question of my character, could you please direct me to the kitchen? I'm starved," she admitted.

And for the second time that day Cleve' s fingers curved around Rina's elbow as he led her across the living room and down a narrow hallway.

"You'll get to meet everyone this weekend. Whitney Hall will be filled with outsiders for the next few months while I select the people who will become members of my campaign team," he explained in a quiet tone.

So the rumors were true. "What about your position as district attorney?" She asked.

"I've taken a leave of absence."

And that meant Cleveland Whitney would be staying at Whitney Hall, she thought. And it also meant he could watch her.

The hall was too narrow for them to walk abreast, so Cleve fell in behind her. She felt the heat of his gaze on her back.

"What are your chances of defeating the incumbent?"

"There's no way Jimmy Ross can stay in office. The man's grossly incompetent," he stated emphatically.

"Incompetent enough to win two terms," she said over her shoulder.

"That may be, but he just lost his godfather. One of my last acts as district attorney was to indict one of his major supporters for bribery and extortion."

"Are you going to try the case?" Rina halted, pressing her back against the wall as Cleve moved past her. His forearm brushed her breast and she felt a jolt of static race throughout her body at the innocent motion. Cleve rested a hand against a swinging door and smiled down at her.

"No. That would be unethical. The press would have a field day, accusing me of pursuing a personal vendetta. I'll defeat Ross with the ballot."

Rina felt the movement of his breathing, and her heart pumped wildly in her chest. Cleveland Whitney was magnetic, compelling and potent.

"You're confident, I have to admire that," she stated hoarsely. She knew it took more than confidence to win an election. It took brains, guile and charm; Cleve had enough of all three to be a formidable opponent.

He flashed his winning smile. "Thank you for the compliment, Miss Matthews."

She nodded. He opened the door, and she stepped into a large kitchen. Abigail and Emily-Jane were seated at a round oak table, while another woman Rina assumed to be Mrs. Bailey filled serving trays with crudités.

"Uncle Cleve, Grandma made me a funny ice cream clown," Emily-Jane squealed excitedly. She waved a spoon filled with chocolate ice cream.

Cleve walked over to the table, leaned over and placed a loud kiss on Emily-Jane's stained, sticky mouth. "Yummy. Em-Jay, you taste fabulous!"

Emily-Jane extended her spoon to Cleve. "Don't eat my mouth. Uncle Cleve. Eat from the spoon."

Rina smiled as Cleve made a big show of eating the ice cream his niece fed him. The child was enchanting. Her hair was styled with four braids, two pinned across the top of her head and two falling to her shoulders. Rina noted the stains of dark chocolate that dotted the child's smooth brown skin when she turned her head.

"Who are you?" Emily-Jane asked boldly. Rina approached the table and stood next to Cleve as Abigail and Cleve hid knowing smiles.

"My name is Rina. What's yours?"

"Emily-Jane Whitney Jackson."

Rina pretended surprise. "You must be very special to have so many names."

Emily-Jane wiped her mouth with a decorative paper napkin. "I have four names because I'm almost four. How old are you?"

Abigail was ready to admonish her granddaughter, but Rina held up a hand. "Twenty-nine."

Emily-Jane's eyebrows wrinkled. "Is that old?"

"Not old at all," Cleve answered for Rina.

The young child stared at Rina. "Are you a princess, Rina? Uncle Cleve says he's going to marry the best, prettiest princess in the whole wide world. Then he would become a king and the princess would be his queen, and they would live happily ever after."

Mrs. Bailey grunted loudly as she continued filling the trays with carrots, celery, radishes and sliced cucumber. "Cleveland Whitney marry? That'll be the day," she mumbled loud enough for everyone to hear. "He's so busy telling that child fairy tales when he knows…"

"If you're finished with that tray I'll take it," Cleve said, preventing Mrs. Bailey from completing her statement.

Mrs. Bailey waved a hand. "Don't worry yourself none about the food. Your mama pays me quite well, thank you, to cook and serve. I'll bring it along directly."

He gave her a murderous look, then turned on his heel and marched stiffly out of the kitchen.

"Essie Bailey," Mrs. Bailey said, acknowledging Rina for the first time.

"Rina Matthews."

Mrs. Bailey looked Rina over with a critical eye, noting the slimness of her waist and narrow hips. "It looks as if you need some of Essie's cooking, girl. You're nothing but skin and bones. Sit yourself down. I saved some dinner for you."

She sat down, smiling at Abigail. It was apparent that Essie Bailey was lord and master of her kitchen, and neither Abigail nor Cleveland dared to usurp her authority.

Mrs. Bailey placed a plate filled with roast chicken, fluffy mashed potatoes and stewed okra on the table in front of Rina.

"She checks the garbage to see if you throw something away," Emily-Jane announced loudly.

"It's a damn shame that you young girls starve yourselves to death just to look pretty," the cook grumbled, picking up her tray. "You hang around here long enough and I'll have you looking real healthy-like." She hoisted the large tray on one hand and headed out of the kitchen through a set of wide swinging doors at the opposite end of the large room.

Abigail's eyes crinkled in amusement. "This is what you'll be living with for the next two months. A cook who runs her kitchen like a storm trooper, a son who feels he must protect his widowed mother and a granddaughter who sees and tells all."

Rina picked up a heavy silver knife and fork and cut into the tender chicken leg. "I don't blame Cleve for trying to protect you," she said before biting into the golden-brown meat.

"Knowing my son, I suppose he's already let you know how he feels about my hiring your company to take over my finances."

"He did not mince words," she admitted. "And neither did I when I told him that I won't tolerate his interference. I work for you, Mrs. Whitney, not Cleveland Whitney."

"Abigail, please." Her dark eyes sparkled brightly as she nodded. "I think Cleveland has finally met his match. I don't know whether it's because he's the oldest child, but he has always been very willful. But then again, he was an only child for eight years and his daddy doted on him. Rubel, Philip and Madeline collectively never challenged me the way Cleveland did and continues to do."

Rina swallowed a mouthful of potatoes. "Willfulness is an essential personality trait for any measure of success in the political arena."

Abigail pushed a glass of water toward Emily-Jane. "I know you're right, Rina, but I don't like politics. Instead of bringing out the best in a person it does the opposite. I feel it reduces people to combatants instead of opponents."

"Cleve should be a very worthy opponent," Rina stated, remembering what Cleve had called her only hours before.

"Cleveland has plenty of time to go into politics," his mother insisted. "At thirty-eight he should be married and enjoying his children. He doesn't need the stress of trying to cure the ills of a large city."

She stared at Abigail. Under the older woman's elegant bearing was a woman, a mother, who still had not accepted her adult son's independence.

"He'll do all right, Abigail."

Abigail's eyebrows shifted. It appeared odd that a young woman who apparently had engaged in a verbal confrontation with Savannah's noted district attorney was defending him to his mother.

"That I have no doubt," Abigail replied quietly. Rina finished her dinner while Abigail helped Emily-Jane from her chair and directed her to the sink to wash the ice cream from her face and hands.

"It's bedtime for you, Emily-Jane," Abigail announced in a soft tone.

Emily-Jane laid her cheek against Abigail's hand. "Can I stay up with Rina, Grandma?"

Rina registered Abigail's glance. "I'm going to bed myself, Emily-Jane. I had a long drive to get here and I'm still tired."

Emily-Jane stuck her thumb in her mouth and trained her large eyes on Rina. "Can you read me a story before you go to bed?"

"Yes," Rina promised.

Emily-Jane smiled around her thumb. "I'm ready to go to bed, Grandma."

Abigail mouthed a "thank you" at Rina.

"Is there a phone I could use?" she asked. "I'd like to call home."

"Of course. There's a phone in the room I've set aside for your office. After Emily-Jane is in bed I'll show you the house," Abigail said, *sotto voce.*

Abigail did not use the narrow hallway to return to the front of the house. They left through the double doors that opened out to a wing where a library and several sitting and reading rooms were located.

Abigail flipped a wall switch in a room, illuminating it with light from a lamp with a crystal base. "This will be your office. I had an electrician check the wiring for the computer you've ordered. I'll be in my bedroom if you need me. It's the third one on the right."

"My room is next to Grandma's," Emily-Jane volunteered.

Rina pulled one of Emily-Jane's braids, smiling at her. "I'll read you a story as soon as I call my father and mother to let them know I'm okay."

"See you later, Rina," Emily-Jane called out as she skipped to her bedroom.

What she hadn't told Emily-Jane was that she had to make not one call, but two. She would call her parents first, then she would call Jason, hoping he would give her the answers she would need to get along with Cleveland Whitney.

CHAPTER 4

Rina examined the room where she would be spending most of her time while auditing Abigail Whitney's holdings. It was nothing like the modern glass and chrome furnishings in the Atlanta office.

Cherry wood chairs covered in pale green brocade, a massive cherry wood desk and writing table, a plush rose-pink carpet, fully leaded lamp bases, and wallpaper in a light green and rose striped pattern hinted of a bygone era, as did sheer pink curtain panels billowing out softly from the open windows.

She sat down on the chair at the desk and lifted an ivory and brass telephone receiver from a gleaming brass cradle. The telephone was the only furnishing in the room that had not been restored to its original state.

Her call was answered after the second ring and Rina spent ten minutes talking to Evelyn and her father. She reassured them both that she wouldn't work too hard, would eat regularly and keep in touch. Ringing off, she dialed Jason's number.

Rina counted off eight rings before depressing the hook and dialing the number to the Atlanta office. The recorded message indicated no one was at the office, so she left her own message, telling Jason to call her at Whitney Hall.

She hung up, a slight frown appearing between her brows. It was after nine and she hadn't expected Jason to be at the office, but she had expected him to activate his answering machine if he wasn't home. Jason Harper was pedantic about not missing telephone calls.

She had to talk to Jason about his meeting with Cleve, but if he wasn't at home or at the office, where was he? Even though Cleve had promised not to inter-fere, Rina did not feel the ease she would have felt with any other client. It was their trust and her confidence that made her work well with every client Harper and Matthews contracted.

She sat at the desk, staring at the patterned wall-paper. The computer company had promised to deliver the equipment she had leased on Monday. That meant she had Thursday and Friday to analyze the financial statements from Abigail's former accountants.

And there was one thing she had promised herself: she would not work weekends. Late January through early May found her putting in six twelve-hour days for sixteen weeks. It was after this grueling schedule that she usually took a vacation. This year was the exception because of the Whitney account.

She left the office and started down the hall to Abigail's room, where she found the older woman pulling a decorative cotton nightgown over Emily-Jane's head.

Emily-Jane wound her chubby arms around Abigail's neck. "Good night. Grandma. I love you."

Abigail returned her granddaughter's noisy kiss. "Good night, precious."

Emily-Jane grabbed a stuffed, floppy-eared rabbit from Abigail's bed and ran to Rina. "I'm ready." She caught Rina's hand, directing her through a connecting dressing room into her own bedroom.

It was a little girl's room, furnished with bleached pine furniture and pink and white accessories. Emily-Jane climbed onto a four-poster bed and pulled a sheet up to her chin. A stack of books lay on a bedside table.

"Which one do you want me to read?" Rina asked, sitting on the rocker next to the bed.

"I want one with a prince and a princess," Emily-Jane mumbled. She had stuck her left thumb in her mouth.

Rina selected one of her own childhood favorites. She inhaled, then let out her breath slowly. The story was one her mother had read to her.

"Once upon a time…"

Rina knew all the words by heart. She read with the cadence Rebecca Matthews had used, her voice rising with excitement and lowering when the prince or princess faced impending danger.

She glanced at Emily-Jane and found her asleep. The thumb was firmly entrenched between her teeth while the rabbit was clutched tightly against the child's rising and falling chest. Rina laid aside the book and leaned over, pressing a light kiss to the little girl's fore-head. Emily-Jane smelled of soap and clean laundry.

Had it been that way for Rebecca? Reading to her daughter then kissing her after she had fallen asleep?

All of her maternal instincts surfaced as she watched Emily-Jane. She and Jason talked about having children, and while she wanted children she wondered if she could have them from a man she loved but was not in love with.

She caught movement out of the corner of her eye and turned. Cleveland Whitney stood in the doorway watching her. Straightening, Rina placed a finger over her lips and walked over to him.

"She's asleep," she whispered.

Cleve nodded and motioned for her to step out of the room. He studied her thoughtfully for a moment. His eyes seemed to undress her as they moved slowly over her face, down to her chest, then back to her face.

Rina silently admired his strong jaw and chin, the flaring nostrils of his straight nose and his wide mouth and lush lips. Cleve's tightly curly black hair was closer cut than Jason's, his features not as refined and his physique larger and bulkier. Whereas Jason was good-looking, Rina saw Cleve as dramatic. If Jason was smooth and polished, Cleve was power and raw sensuality. She felt the power in his walk and in his gestures; she knew instinctively that Cleve was in control at all times.

Lowering his chin, he glared at her. "Whenever Em-Jay stays over I read to her before she goes to sleep."

She was stunned by this announcement. He was jealous. Cleveland Whitney was put out because she had usurped his nightly ritual with his niece.

She patted his hard shoulder in a comforting gesture. "You can have her tomorrow," Rina said softly. "Good night, Cleve." She walked several feet to Abigail's room, leaving him staring at her back. Abigail glanced up from the newspaper she had been reading when Rina entered her bedroom. She removed a pair of half-glasses and placed them on a bedside table.

At sixty-two, Abigail Whitney was still a very attractive, vibrant woman. Her silver hair blended softly with tobacco-gold smooth skin and large, intelligent, dark eyes, like Cleve's eyes, which sparkled like brilliant onyx.

"That was quick," Abigail remarked.

"She was asleep before I reached the part where the prince rescues the princess," she explained.

Abigail rose from an antique rocker, smiling. "It must be your soft, soothing voice. Cleveland usually reads two before she falls asleep."

A slight smile curved Rina's mouth. Again she had managed to infiltrate Cleve's sphere of influence with his family. The smile vanished quickly. Instinctively she knew she would pay for her actions. Somehow she knew Cleve would not be a gracious loser.

Arm-in-arm Abigail led Rina through connecting hallways, passages and more rooms than Rina could count.

"When Noah Whitney purchased this property it had been part of a fifty-thousand-acre plantation," Abigail explained. "The former owners had a self-sustaining empire with a brick kiln, cotton gin, ice-house, blacksmith shop and leather tannery. Now we only have two hundred acres, but nowadays it's more than enough to maintain."

"'You're fortunate to have retained so many of the original furnishings," Rina remarked, running her fingers over the smooth marble on the mantel of a fireplace.

"Not every piece came with the house," Abigail stated in a reverent tone. "Subsequent Whitneys fell on hard times and had to sell off priceless heirlooms in exchange for food. It was only after the turn of the century that the Whitneys began to rebuild their empire. They set up their own insurance company, selling policies to black folks because the white companies refused to cover them. Then a set of twin brothers received a charter from the state and established a bank. Several cousins went into publishing with the *Savannah Free Press,* and in the early fifties Boyd and his brother bought their first radio station."

She registered the huskiness in Abigail's voice when she mentioned her late husband's name. "How did you meet Boyd Whitney?" she questioned.

Abigail steered Rina over to a mustard-gold velvet settee in the room the Whitneys referred to as the breakfast room. Its many windows faced east, permitting unlimited light during the early morning hours.

An elegant embroidered tablecloth and matching napkins covered a table large enough to seat a dozen. A buffet server and breakfront in a Chippendale design held translucent china, fragile crystal and sterling silver serving pieces.

"I met Boyd at a Whitney black and white ball," Abigail began. "I was engaged to another boy at the time, but somehow that meant nothing to Boyd."

Rina's eyebrows arched at this disclosure. "How did you break your engagement?"

Abigail smothered a laugh. "Boyd did it for me. A week following the ball he called my parents and invited himself to Sunday dinner. After dinner we sat on the porch and Boyd told me that he was going to marry me. I laughed and he didn't. He called again the next week. We eloped on our first date."

Her low laugh joined Abigail's light titter. "Good for him," she replied. "The man knew what he wanted and went after it."

"Boyd was successful because he never permitted anyone to define his limits."

Like Cleve, she thought.

Abigail's expression stilled, growing serious. "It's amazing that Cleveland is so much like his father," she mused aloud, reading Rina's thoughts. "Once he decides on a course of action, nothing will stop him. All of his life he's been a winner. He graduated at the top of his class in high school, college and at law school. He's won every case he's brought to trial." She shook her head. "He doesn't know how to lose, Rina."

Rina reached over and squeezed Abigail's fingers gently. "He'll survive even if he doesn't win the election."

"How can you be that certain?"

"Because he's a survivor."

"Are you?" Abigail queried, giving Rina a penetrating look.

She released Abigail's hands and stood up. Walking over to one of the many windows, Rina stared out at the shadowy outline of trees and shrubs.

"My mother died when I was eight." She swallowed back the sob in her voice. "I thought I wanted to be buried with her until I realized my father would be left alone." Turning, she faced Abigail. "I needed my father and he needed me. So I survived, for both of us. Cleve will also find a special someone who'll be there to help him through his losses and disappointments."

Abigail smiled again. "Are you certain you're only twenty-nine, Rina? You sound as if you've inherited an old spirit."

Rina returned her smile. "You sound like my grandmother. She claimed that I'd inherited a spirit from someone who lived a hundred years ago."

Abigail regarded her with a speculative stare. "Have you set your wedding date?"

The query startled her. She had not disclosed to Abigail that she was to announce her engagement to Jason after she returned to Atlanta, and that meant Jason must have mentioned it to her.

"No, I haven't."

"I suppose you'll know when it's the right time." Abigail rose to her feet. "This old lady is going to call it a day. I'm hosting a luncheon for my bridge club tomorrow, and I'm going to need all of my strength to deal with those ladies. Do you remember how to find your way back to your room?" Rina nodded. "By the way, Rina, you're invited to the ball."

A warning voice whispered in her head with Abigail's invitation. Jason would be expected to attend as her date. Could she hope to avoid a hostile confrontation if and when Jason and Cleve met again? Straightening out the Whitney matriarch's finances was easy; convincing Cleve to trust her partner wasn't.

She followed Abigail out of the breakfast room and managed to find the kitchen without getting lost. She poured a glass of milk from a bottle in the walk-in refrigerator, drinking it quickly before retracing her steps through the narrow hallway to the wing of the house where her bedroom was located. A sliver of light showed under the door in the room off the living room, and a low babble of voices replaced the raucous laughter she had heard earlier that evening.

She made it to her bedroom, pushed open the door and encountered muted light from a lamp that threw long and short shadows on whitewashed walls. It wasn't the warmth of the room's interior that held her rapt attention but that of a single snow-white rose on the pillow on her bed.

Someone had been in her room.

Walking over to the dresser, Rina noted her handbag, keys, credit card case and loose change had not been moved. She went back to the bed and picked up the flower. All of the thorns had been removed, though droplets of moisture still clung to the velvet petals, indicating the rose had been recently cut.

Pressing her nose to the opening bud, Rina inhaled its heady fragrance. She would thank Abigail for the thoughtful gesture in the morning.

She found a glass in the bathroom and filled it with water, placing the rose in it. She then went through the nightly ablution of washing her face and brushing her teeth.

She slipped out of her slacks, blouse and underwear and picked up the nightgown at the foot of the bed. Minutes later she lay on the crisp sheets, staring up at the exposed beams on the ceiling, reassessing her first day at Whitney Hall.

She closed her eyes and Cleve's face surfaced in her mind. Her lids flew up and she knew she had to call on all of her resolve to not fall under the dynamic vitality Cleveland Whitney exuded. Reaching over, she flicked off the lamp, and the room was plunged in darkness.

Sleep was elusive that night. And as the moon was overshadowed by a brighter sphere, Rina found no solace in sleep, for her dreams were filled with a man who chased her relentlessly. She did not recognize him, but then she did not stop, in fear that he would capture her.

Her foot caught in an exposed root and she fell. Within seconds the man's body covered hers. Rina felt his hot breath on her neck and his hands as they swept over her body. She opened her mouth to scream, but all sound vanished as his mouth covered hers, searching, sucking and drawing from her what she had not thought possible, unbridled passion. Everything within her reacted to his exploration of her mouth and body. Fire burned out of control, soft moans escaped her parted lips, and waves of undulating ecstasy washed over her.

He raised his head and she reached out to touch his face, but then he faded. Like a wisp of smoke, he disappeared, leaving her aching and craving his touch.

The shock of losing him woke her. Moisture lathered her body as blood coursed through her veins like molten lava. Rina's trembling fingers touched her moist lips, her breath coming in short gasps.

"It was only a dream," she whispered breathlessly in the silence of the room.

It had been an illusion, but her body had reacted violently. Her response to the erotic fantasy was too real, too unsettling to dismiss.

Closing her eyes, Rina suffered the aftermath of her traitorous body. She didn't trust herself to go back to sleep and relive the erotic fantasy, so she lay in the bed and waited for dawn. With the light she could live in a real world with real images. The dark hid a secret longing she didn't want to acknowledge.

CHAPTER 5

Rina walked into the kitchen. "Good morning, Mrs. Bailey." Essie Bailey offered Rina a rare smile. "Good morning. I see you're an early riser." She beat an egg mixture with a wire whisk. "Are you ready for breakfast?"

"My breakfast is usually a cup of coffee."

Mrs. Bailey shook her head. Her salt and pepper gray hair was pulled back into a bun and covered with a net. "You're not going to get away with having coffee for breakfast around here. So you'd just better get that notion out of your head." The rising color in Mrs. Bailey's face was more than the heat from the range. "Now, you just get your hips into the breakfast room and eat. Go!" she ordered when Rina didn't move.

"Yes, ma'am," she mumbled obediently. *She's a tyrant,* Rina thought as she made her way to the breakfast room. *Was there anyone at Whitney Hall who defied Essie Bailey?*

Bright sunshine and Cleve's presence greeted her as she walked into the breakfast room. His back was to Rina, so he did not see her appreciative perusal of his powerful legs in a pair of tan walking shorts.

"Good morning, Rina."

She started. "Do you have eyes in the back of your head?"

He turned slowly, flashing his winning smile. "No. I detected your perfume. The fragrance is very distinctive and memorable. Like its wearer," he added.

"Thank you." His compliment caught her off guard. She walked across the room and stood beside Cleve at the buffet server. Mouth-watering smells seeped from under the lids of silver serving dishes. "Mrs. Bailey chased me out of her kitchen."

"She's a culinary despot," Cleve spat out.

"Why do you keep her?"

"She's the best cook in the state."

"That's reason enough to keep her," she concurred.

Cleve uncovered a dish, then picked up a plate. "It looks as if we have grits." He uncovered another serving dish. "Ham, bacon and sausage."

Rina uncovered several. "This one has pancakes and waffles. There're also scrambled eggs." She glanced up at Cleve. "How many is she cooking for?"

"We have a few overnight guests. What can I serve you?" Cleve stared down at Rina, noting the dark shadows under her eyes that had not been there the day before. He also noted the lighter strands of gold curls in her hair, still damp from her morning shower.

"Rough night?" he asked knowingly.

"Strange bed."

"You'll get used to it," he said in a quiet tone.

Her gaze moved to his strong throat, revealed by the open collar of a pale blue denim shirt. "I'm sure I will."

"Sometimes a nightcap of bourbon helps," Cleve volunteered.

"I prefer milk," she countered.

He shrugged his shoulders. "It was only a suggestion."

"And I thank you for your suggestion."

Cleve put the plate down and turned back to her. "Do you always have to have the last word, Rina?"

"No, I don't." Her hands went to her hips. "All I did was thank you for your suggestion."

"And I thank you for your suggestion," he repeated, mimicking her.

Rina threw her hands up in disgust. "What's your problem, counselor? Am I on trial? Must I analyze everything I say before saying it?"

"No!" Cleve shouted.

"Then get off my back," she retorted, her eyes blazing with angry green lights. "I'm not going away, Cleveland Whitney. I'm not going to disappear because you will it. I have a project to complete, and no one will stop me from doing what I've been contracted to do."

Cleve applauded slowly. "Bravo, Ms. Matthews. You just showed me that you still have a lot to learn about the cutthroat world of business. I just bested you because you permitted yourself to get personal. You were much better yesterday."

Rina swallowed back her anger and embarrassment, deciding to join Cleve at his own game. "Try
me again when I've had more than two hours of unin-
terrupted sleep."

Cleve reached out, touching the tiny gold locket
resting between her breasts over a crisp white camp
shirt. "You're on," he crooned softly, accepting her
challenge.

"Good morning."

Cleve and Rina sprang apart guiltily.

"Good morning, Mother."

"Good morning, Abigail."

They had spoken in unison.

Rina reached across Cleve and handed him a plate.
"I'd like grits, eggs and bacon, please." She smiled at
Abigail. "What can I serve you?"

Abigail selected whole-wheat pancakes and a link
of beef sausage. Her eyes shifted from Rina to Cleve
as they stood together at the buffet table and registered something they failed to recognize from the very
beginning.

"Coffee or tea, Mother?"

Abigail took a seat at the head of the table. "Tea,
please, Cleveland."

Cleve placed Rina's plate in front of her when she
sat. "And you?"

She flashed a saccharin smile. "Coffee, please, sir."

Cleve expertly balanced both cups and his plate. "I
waited table at college," he explained when Rina
raised her eyebrows at his dexterity. "My allowance

was never enough, so I worked at a restaurant to supplement my meager income." He sat down opposite her, winking. "Did you work your way through college?"

"No. I lived at home."

"Daddy didn't trust his little girl to leave home?" Cleve teased.

Her fingers tightened on her fork as she glared across the table. "Not going away was my decision."

"Oh really," he replied facetiously. "Daddy really spoiled you, didn't he?"

"Of course he did," Rina confirmed. "He always made certain I got what I wanted."

"Even now?"

She broke off a portion of bacon and picked it up with long slender fingers. "Not any longer. It's Jason who now gives me everything I want." Rina knew she had hit a raw nerve. Cleve stiffened as if she had struck him.

"What about your needs, Rina? Does Harper take care of all your needs, too?"

It was as if they were the only two in the room. The air was thick, radiating with checked emotions, emotions as volatile and erratic as an impending summer storm.

Cleve's gaze was bold, dropping from her face to her breasts and she understood his double meaning instantly.

"Cleveland," Abigail whispered.

"Let her answer, Mother," he countered.

"I'm not going to let you bully her," Abigail replied.

"It's all right, Abigail," Rina cut in. She knew it had progressed beyond a game; it now was personal. She had to stand up to Cleve or he would verbally destroy her.

"The answer is yes," she stated in a tone filled with confidence. "Jason takes care of all my needs."

Cleve picked up his cup, smiling at her over the rim. "I'll ask you the same question at the end of your stay, and well see if your answer will be the same."

The banked fires Rina saw in his eyes sent ripples of delicious heat throughout her body, for despite their vying repartee a thread of veiled sexual attraction had been obvious from their initial encounter.

She pulled her brilliant gaze away from his smug expression. She had no intention of falling under Cleve's magnetic spell. She was involved with Jason, and there was no room in her life for another man.

She made it through breakfast, directing most of her remarks to Abigail. Cleve elected not to comment when she asked Abigail about her involvement with various societies and organizations.

She concluded, saying, "After I examine your tax returns and analyze your financial statements I'll have a better view of what to recommend for investment and philanthropic purposes."

"That sounds wonderful," Abigail replied. "I detest discussing and handling money. That's why I've always hired someone to take care of everything for me."

"I won't promise miracles, but do my best," Rina said. She drained her second cup of coffee. "If you'll excuse me, I'd like to begin working." She smiled at Cleve. "Thank you for your company this morning, Mr. Whitney."

Cleve slouched down in his chair, crossing thick arms over his chest. He grunted softly, giving her a perceptible nod. "We must do this again."

She pushed back from the table. "Dining or sparring?" Abigail hid a smile behind her napkin.

"Both," Cleve replied, his eyes widening with anticipation.

Rina wrinkled her nose. "I'll think about it." She was barely out of the room when she heard Abigail's voice. She could not hear what Abigail was saying to Cleve, but whatever it was, it was angry and strident.

Rina sat at the desk in the sitting-room-turned-office, staring down at the neat rows of figures and percentages lining a columnar analysis pad.

She took a quick glance at her watch. The morning had slipped by quickly. She always lost track of time whenever she was involved in an auditing project; and it was almost noon and Jason had not returned her call. She combed her fingers through the thick mane of curly hair that fell to her shoulders.

Anger and anxiety spurted through her as her fingers drummed nervously on the desktop. Seconds later she picked up the telephone and dialed the Atlanta office.

"Good morning. Harper and Matthews," came a pleasantly modulated voice.

Rina took a deep breath. "Good morning, Aimee."

"Hello, Rina. How are you? How was the drive down?"

"Everything went well."

"Tell me, Rina. Is he hot?"

Her brow furrowed. "Who?"

"Cleveland Whitney. Did you meet him?" Aimee's professional telephone manner evaporated quickly.

She smiled at the receptionist's designation for men. Either they were hot or cold, never lukewarm. "Yes, I met him."

"Well, is he as hot as everyone says he is?"

"He's quite attractive, Aimee," she admitted honestly. "Did Jason get my message?" Rina asked, changing the topic smoothly.

"I gave it to him when he came in this morning," Aimee confirmed.

A tremor of annoyance pricked her. Jason should have returned her call. "Is he in?"

Aimee recognized the change in her boss's tone. "I'll put you through to him. Take care of yourself, Rina."

"You too." Rina's fingers resumed their staccato tapping as she waited for Jason to pick up her call.

"Hey, baby."

She ignored the irritating endearment Jason insisted on calling her. "Why didn't you return my call?"

A low, soothing chuckle came through the wire. "Come on, Rina, lighten up, you're supposed to be on vacation."

"This is not a vacation, Jason."

"Try to think of it as one, Rina," Jason retorted, his normally soft tone vanishing.

"You think of it as one because I can't. What I want to know is, what did you say to Cleveland Whitney to make him so suspicious of us?"

There was a pregnant pause before Jason spoke again. "That's between Whitney and me."

"Wrong, Jason. It involves me because I am here. I see the man, eat at his table and sleep under his roof. I have enough work to do without having to deal with Cleve and his suspicions."

"I told him in no uncertain terms that you belong to me, Rina," Jason admitted. "Whitney had no problem understanding that our relationship extends beyond this office."

"You didn't tell him that," she whispered, choking on her own words.

She felt a lump rise in her throat. Jason had flaunted their relationship, their private lives. When had he become so insecure?

"Rina?" came Jason's voice when she didn't speak.

"Yes, Jason." The two words were impersonal, cold.

"Come on, baby. You can't blame me for being a little jealous. You know that I love you," he crooned.

He loved her; loved her so much that he had humiliated her; loved her so much that he hadn't bothered to call to see whether she had arrived safely; loved her so much that he hadn't returned her phone call.

"Look, Jason, I have to get back to work. I'll call you in a few days."

"Rina…"

Whatever Jason was going to say was cut off as she replaced the receiver on its cradle. Biting down hard on her lower lip, she blinked back angry tears. In less than twenty-four hours her whole life had been turned upside down.

The man she had planned to marry had stripped her bare, exposing her to a man who disturbed her more than she was willing to admit.

Since meeting Cleveland Whitney, she discovered what had been missing in her relationship with Jason: passion.

Even when she and Cleve were trading vicious barbs, there was a slow burning flame between them, threatening to spread and burn out of control.

Had Cleve also felt the heat?

Rina stood up and walked over to a window. Pushing her hands into the large pockets of her loose-fitting white cotton slacks, she surveyed the meticulously manicured flower garden at Whitney Hall.

Her gaze fell on a bush of delicate white roses, reminding her of the bud left on her pillow the night before. The sight of the flowers brought back flashes of her dream. The stranger had made love to her in a garden of white roses.

She shook her head, hoping to rid her mind of the erotic fantasy. Was it wishful thinking? Had she fantasized about Cleve making love to her? Did she want him to make love to her? Or better, did she need him to make love to her?

She dismissed her traitorous musings, walking out of the room. She had to go for a walk or swim, anything but sit and think about Cleveland Whitney.

CHAPTER 6

Rina made her way across the living room floor, now covered with a protective tarp. The space was a beehive of activity as two men slowly lowered the massive chandelier to the floor at the center of the living room under the watchful eyes of a petite woman dressed in a pale pink uniform that distinguished her as part of the domestic staff. Two other men were moving about the fourth-floor octagon, manipulating hand-held vacuum wands, picking up the fine layer of dust from the elaborately decorated ceiling.

She nodded at another young man who gave her a friendly smile. Whitney Hall was being refurbished for the upcoming black and white ball.

Opening the front door, she stepped out into the sultry heat. Whitney Hall's thick walls and shuttered windows kept out the day's intense heat, while opened windows at night availed its spacious interiors of cooling ocean breezes.

She made her way across the circular drive and around the side of the house, returning a smile from the wizened old gardener pruning azaleas. The all-encompassing beauty of the grounds surrounding

Whitney Hall astounded Rina as she noted the neatly manicured lawns, wisteria, oak and dogwood trees and the boxwood and vegetable gardens and orchards.

She followed a flagstone walk, then turned and stared back at the exquisite structure filled with history and tradition. The building looked perfectly square on the exterior while the interior appeared eight-sided because of the octagonal upper floors.

Rina continued along curving stone steps that narrowed as towering trees and shrubs threatened to reclaim the land, returning it to its natural untamed wilderness.

She felt her tension easing as she lost herself to the beauty of her surroundings. A slight breeze rustled the branches of a fruit tree, and its snowy blossoms floated down, settling on her hair like a transparent white lace wedding veil.

A tiny snake slithered over the toes of her espadrilles, stopping her momentarily. The earth-colored reptile retreated quickly under a pile of decaying leaves and wilting flowers.

The woods thinned and the distinctive smell of salt water stung her nostrils. Rina felt the full strength of the noonday summer sun the moment she left the woods. Sand grated under her feet and gently waving sea oats heralded her approach to the wide expanse of the Atlantic Ocean stretching eastward. A thick haze had almost obscured the outline of nearby Sapelo Island.

Blue-gray waves rose and crested as the incoming tide deposited its treasures on the wet sand. She played a nimble game of tag with the surf, leaving her footprints in the sand before they were washed away forever.

She ignored the cold water seeping into her shoes as she stood facing the untamed ocean, peering out at its endless unseen boundaries.

Transfixed by the graceful moves of circling gulls as they sailed the wind currents, dipping and soaring above the gentle waves in search of food, Rina laughed aloud when she spied a crab trying to escape to the safety of the ocean's depths before the gulls turned it into a succulent meal.

Rina walked several miles down the beach, stopping twice to sit on the sand and watch the waves rise higher and higher. The hot sun darkened her skin and brightened the gold in her hair, while she feasted on the cooling ocean breezes and luxuriated in the healing rays of the sun.

Only when she noticed dark clouds dotting the horizon did she make an attempt to return to Whitney Hall and Cleveland Whitney; she had to talk to Cleve about Jason. She had to clear the air and dispel the tension between them.

The sky had darkened ominously, nearly obscuring the afternoon sun as Rina quickened her pace. The outline of the house came into view with the first rumble of thunder that shook the earth. The flagstone steps along the path glistened like large, silver shields as lightning rent the heavens, followed by awesome, ear-shattering thunder.

She made it to the house as the first large drops splattered the rich earth. Removing her shoes, she made her way across the living room. The workmen were gone, the house unnaturally quiet.

She climbed the staircase to the second floor, walking along the hallway past Whitneys staring at her from vibrantly painted canvases in gilded frames. She wondered if they saw her as an intruder or as a friend, because she was certain their present-day heir saw her as the former.

She walked into her bedroom, unbuttoning her blouse at the same time. It was when she slipped out of her slacks that she saw it. There was another white rose on her pillow.

Approaching the bed slowly, heart pounding loudly, Rina stared at the flower. Like the first one, the thorns had been removed. Instinctively she knew Abigail had not left the flower. Had it been Cleve?

Why a rose? she thought. *Was it a peace offering? Or a gesture of...*

No, she thought, shaking her head. Why was she entertaining fantasies when she was a realist? But then wasn't her dream of being chased by a mysterious man an illusion? And hadn't the man made love to her, and hadn't she responded with a passion she never thought herself capable of giving?

Her gaze shifted to the other rose, now fully opened and filling the room with its distinctively sweet fragrance. Shock upon shock assailed her senses. A slender, gracefully curving crystal vase had replaced the water tumbler. Whoever had left the rose had given her an additional gift of an exquisite vase.

Rina spun around and stared at the door to the bedroom. There was a key in the lock, but she did not want to use it. She did not want to thwart her mystery visitor, not until she discovered who he or she was.

Picking up the rose, she placed it with the other in the vase, then headed for the bathroom. She needed a bath to soothe her hot flesh and wash away the grains of sand sticking to her legs and feet.

Filling the antique claw-foot bathtub with warm water, she added a thick, rich bath oil, stripped off her clothes then settled down in a frothy cloud of fragrant bubbles.

Outdoors the sky blackened and the wind screamed its fury only moments before the storm broke, lashing Whitney Hall with a relentless driving rain. She closed her eyes and willed her mind to go blank.

Twenty minutes later, the water cooled, the bubbles disappeared and the storm subsided, leaving only a steady tapping sound against the windows. Rina stepped out of the tub, wrapping a thick bath sheet around her body.

She returned to the bedroom and lit one of the large scented candles on the mantel over the fireplace. The space was washed with calm, golden light. The flickering flame threw long and short shadows on the whitewashed ceiling and walls and the massive pieces of furniture.

She tried imagining living at Whitney Hall years before the advent of electric lights and indoor plumbing. Household servants would be responsible for lighting the myriad candles in the chandelier in the living room as well as the many other rooms in the elegant mansion. One could not turn on a faucet for water, but gallons upon gallons would be hauled from the outside up the back stairs for a treasured bath.

She smiled, thinking of the formally dressed men and women preening in their silken finery. It would have been very much a fairy tale existence, she mused. Smoothing a silky perfumed body lotion onto her own arms and legs she thought of the preparations for the black and white ball she had been invited to attend.

As it had been more than one hundred years before, the house would be filled with people of color in their formal attire. Beautiful women with expanses of smooth, glowing skin in hues ranging from satiny cream to dewy velvet black would entice and delight the naked eye. Men in white dinner jackets or varying styles of the familiar tuxedo would pose elegantly, handsomely, while paying homage to their adoring partners.

The Whitney black and white ball was a part of Georgia's history, and Rina was going to become a thread in the fabric of that history for the first time.

She mentally calculated the number of weeks before the event. It was always held the first Saturday in August, which meant she had less than two months to find something appropriate to wear. She knew a trip to Savannah was necessary if she wanted a ball gown.

The clock on the mantel chimed softly and she glanced up. It was only three-thirty. Abigail had informed her that breakfast and lunch were always informal; however, dinner was a sit-down affair and always served promptly at seven. It was too late for lunch and much too early for dinner.

Rina did not feel hungry, so she decided to spend some time reading one of the many books she had found in the delightfully romantic bedroom. She pulled an oversized T-shirt over her head and walked over to a built-in bookcase. Running her finger along the hardcover spines of a collection of Frank Yerby novels, she selected one she hadn't read: *The Golden Hawk*.

Returning to her bed, she fluffed up the pillows behind her head, turned on the bedside lamp and was soon engrossed in the adventures of Yerby's Kit Gerado. She read until the clock chimed six-thirty, and it was with a great deal of reluctance that she put the book aside to get dressed for dinner.

Rina slipped into a pair of dark green satin bikini underpants and a matching strapless lacy bra. She stepped into a jade and white batik print cotton sundress with narrow straps crisscrossing her back, smoothing out the fitted bodice over her breasts and waist. She brushed her hair, securing it with an elastic band on the top of her head. Three large tortoise-shell pins were fitted into a neat twist of sun-lightened hair.

Sitting at the dressing table, she applied streaks of pearly terra cotta beige and muted pistachio color to her lids, a light coat of night-green mascara to her lashes and a luminous, shimmering apricot color to her mouth. With a large sable brush, she dusted her cheeks and forehead with a loose bronze powder giving her flawless complexion a rich, metallic glow which enhanced the brilliant green flecks in her clear gray-brown eyes.

Rina pushed her slender feet into a pair of low-heel bone-colored pumps, then reached for a matching jacket to the sundress. She flicked off the lamp on the dressing table and blew out the candle. The fragrance of lemon-scented wax and the cloying aroma of the roses lingered in the space as she left the room, closing the door behind her. The hands of the delicate gold watch on her wrist indicated she would be on time for dinner.

Her light step took her down the curving staircase, across the living room and into the dining room. The clock on the fireplace mantel chimed the hour. She stared at the gleaming surface of the cherry wood table, puzzled. It had not been set for dining. Turning, she made her way to the kitchen.

Cleve glanced up from shredding salad greens, smiling at her the moment he detected her presence.

"It's just the two of us tonight," he informed her, noting her startled expression. "Mrs. Bailey is off until Saturday, and Mother and Em-Jay went out for dinner."

She entered the kitchen, returning Cleve's smile. "Do you need help?"

Cleve's eyebrows inched up in surprise. "You cook?" he teased.

Her smile faded, but she caught it before it curved into a frown. "Who do you think feeds me?"

"Your boyfriend," he drawled, his voice low, the tone sarcastic. "Didn't you tell me that he takes care of all of your needs?"

"Not that one," Rina retorted softly.

"He can't cook?"

Bits of green clung to Cleve's fingers as he stopped shredding and stared at her, his gaze caressing her face and body.

"Then you cook for him?"

"No." She had to talk to Cleve about Jason, but not about what Jason did for her or what she did for Jason.

"I spoke to my partner this afternoon," she began, watching Cleve slice radishes into thin pieces. "I'd like to apologize for him."

"Why should you?" Cleve concentrated on wielding the sharp knife. "Harper is responsible for his own actions, Rina. In case you haven't noticed, he's supposed to be a man, not a boy. Women don't apologize for men, or vice versa."

Rina felt her face heat up. "You don't understand…"

"What the hell is there to understand, Rina?" Cleve put down the knife, glaring at her. "The man doesn't know me that well, yet he has the unmitigated gall to threaten me. And I don't like threats, Miss Rina Matthews. Not from anyone."

Jason hadn't told her that he had threatened Cleve. He had acted like a spoiled child, no, a little boy. The heat in her face added color to her features.

Cleve must have registered her embarrassment, saying, "You deserve a lot better than Harper."

Was Cleve telling her what she hadn't wanted to believe? He had known her for less than twenty-four hours, yet Cleveland Whitney was echoing what her father had been telling her for a long time now.

When had she become so complacent in her relationship with Jason? Had she, like so many other women, lapsed into a habit of acceptance because Jason was comfortable, familiar, and it was easier to accept what she had rather than look for someone better?

But Rina had to admit to herself that her future with Jason was tenuous, and Cleve's assessment of their personal relationship added confusion to her already tormented emotions.

"Do you think you're more deserving than Jason?" The words were out before she could stop them.

Cleve picked up a terrycloth towel and wiped his hands, a maddening smile parting his lips. "I'd never treat you as shabbily as Harper does," he replied, not answering her query. "If you were mine, Rina, I would make certain you would never need another man."

His gaze and the timbre of his voice sent shivers of fire and ice throughout her body. Her whole being was trembling, poised and waiting, and Rina could feel the force of the sexual magnetism that made Cleveland Whitney the confident man he was.

Naked desire leapt into his eyes, and she recognized it immediately. "How?" she challenged, her voice low and husky.

Cleve took three steps, bringing him inches from her. He was surprised when she didn't take a backwards step. The forefinger of his right hand touched the curve of a sculpted cheekbone, inching slowly down to her mouth. He applied the slightest pressure to her lips before dropping his hand.

His eyes never wavered as they held her steady gaze. When it appeared that neither would back down, he said, "I'd have to show you, Rina."

Her tongue wet her lower lip, drawing his gaze to the spot. "I think not," she replied, "because you'll never get that opportunity."

He concealed his anger well. Rina knew she had struck a raw nerve. She had challenged his manhood.

Cleve went back to the cooking island, picking up the knife. He dropped it with a loud gasp. Blood spurted from a deep gash along his palm.

She was stunned by the curses he mumbled savagely under his breath. The butcher-block counter was quickly stained with droplets of bright red. She was galvanized into action, her slender fingers holding his wrist while she wrapped his injured hand in the towel.

Cleve went rigid. "Don't touch me," he snapped through clenched teeth.

Rina pulled him toward the sink. "Stops acting like a baby, Cleveland. Hold it under the cold water while I get some ice from the refrigerator."

A quick jerk of his arm and Rina fell against his chest. Her hands went to his shoulders as she tried regaining her balance, while Cleve's left arm curved around her waist, molding her to the length of his body.

"It's only a little cut," he mumbled, lowering his head until their mouths were inches apart.

Rina was trapped by an arm of steel and hypnotized by Cleve's blatant virility. "You're bleeding," she said slowly.

"It's nothing."

Her pulse quickened. "Please, Cleve."

His gaze widened, taking in her increased breathing and the deepening color in her cheeks. "Please what?"

She could not ignore the solid feel of his chest against her breasts. The thin fabric of his shirt failed to trap the heat from his body, and his warmth penetrated the cotton of her dress and jacket.

"Please what, Rina?" Cleve repeated. She dared not move. The urge to curve her arms around Cleve's neck and pull his head down was as powerful as the moon's effect on the tide; she wanted to taste his mouth; she wanted to taste his jaw and throat; she wanted to bare her body and experience the thrill of naked flesh touching, everywhere; she wanted to surrender all of herself to this man, a stranger, holding back nothing,

But she wouldn't, she couldn't.

"Please take care of your hand," she finally said.

Cleve pulled back slightly. "You don't want me to let you go?" He was smiling.

Rina tilted her chin, returning his smile. "If you take care of your hand, you'll have to let me go."

Cleve released her and turned back to the sink. He didn't hear her audible sigh of relief as cold water flowed from the faucet. Rina managed to make it to the refrigerator on trembling legs and fill a glass with a few cubes from the automatic icemaker.

She stared at Cleve's tailored navy blue slacks and white shirt, with a faint navy pinstripe, as he stood at the sink, examining his hand. There was no doubt that those slacks had not come off a department store rack. The garment had been tailored to fit the length of his legs, waist and hips with detailed precision.

She returned to his side and reached for his hand. His large, well-groomed fingers were cradled in her smaller hand as she held a cube of ice against an inch-long gash on the fleshy heel of his broad palm. Cleve's warm breath skipped along her ear and cheek.

"Do you think I'll live?" he teased.

She applied more pressure with the ice. She tilted her head, smiling up at him. "Do you want my professional opinion?" He returned her smile and nodded. She wrinkled her nose. "You have a better than one hundred percent chance of surviving, Mr. Whitney."

Cleve took a deep breath, inhaling the seductive fragrance of her perfume. He examined the natural curve of her arching brows, the sweep of thick, dark, gold-tipped lashes and the graceful curve of her cheekbones. "You're an incredibly beautiful woman, Rina Matthews," he stated reverently. He continued to study her profile as she turned her head. "I envy Jason Harper."

"You shouldn't," she retorted quickly, turning back to face him.

"Why not?"

"You're Cleveland Whitney, the youngest and most popular D.A. in Savannah's history. And early next year you may be sworn in as one of its youngest mayors. Aren't you aware that you're the consummate mover and shaker?"

Cleve shrugged broad shoulders. "I'm not talking about politics, Rina. I make it a point never to mix business with my personal affairs."

She stiffened as if she had been shot. "Touché, Cleve."

His free hand moved quickly, to hold her hand that cradled his injured one. "I'm sorry, Rina." His tone indicated he was sincere.

Rina extracted her hand from his and dropped the melting sliver of ice into the sink. "I think it would be better for the both of us if we do not discuss Jason Harper."

Cleve examined the gash, which had stopped bleeding. "I agree."

She sighed in relief. Not having Jason to verbally kick around would dispel a lot tension between them. Getting Cleve to trust her was another matter, a matter she was confident she would resolve easily.

"Do you have a first-aid kit?" she asked.

"It'll be all right."

"Get the kit, Cleve," Rina ordered.

He folded his arms over his chest, holding the injured hand away from his shirt. "Damn, but you're bossy. You like giving orders, don't you?"

"No more than you do," she countered.

He stared at her solemn expression, then burst into laughter. "I think I've met my match with you, Rina Matthews. We're going to have fun, Rina. Lots of fun. I'll let you finish up your Florence Nightingale skills, then we'll go out for dinner."

"Aren't you going to cook?" Rina questioned.

"Are you?" he returned, dropping his chin and staring at her from lowered lids. He held up his right hand. "I'm going on the disabled list. So that leaves you to do the cooking."

Rina shook her head. "Not."

He flashed a saccharin grin. "Then we dine out."

CHAPTER 7

Cleve escorted Rina to his car, having added a navy and white-striped silk tie and an eggshell white linen jacket as a concession to their dining out.

The rain stopped as he assisted her into the silver BMW coupe. The bandage on his hand gleamed like a beacon in the auto's dim interior.

"What's your preference, Rina?" Cleve questioned as he started up the car.

"Seafood."

He smiled. "I was hoping you would say that."

He rested his injured right hand on a thigh, maneuvering the steering wheel with his left. Rina suspected he was undergoing some discomfort.

She glanced at his strong profile. "We have something in common."

"What's that?" he asked, not taking his gaze off the road.

"We both like fish."

"I suspect we have a lot more in common than an affinity for fish."

She settled back against the leather seat. "Music?"

"Jazz."

"Classical," she countered.

"Color?" Cleve asked.

"White."

"That's not a color, Rina."

"Green."

"Bingo," Cleve confirmed. "Season."

"Winter."

"Christmas?"

"Especially Christmas," Rina replied.

"Not bad, Rina. We like fish, the color green, winter and Christmas. Do you like children?"

"Yes."

"Do you want children?"

"Yes."

"What's your favorite gemstone?"

"Pearls."

"I had you figured for diamonds." He took a quick glance at her ringless fingers.

"Only if they're paired with emeralds."

Cleve nodded. "Of course. A green stone. Favorite sport?"

"Swimming. I try to swim at least twice a week."

"Where do you swim?"

"At an Atlanta health club."

"Nothing beats the ocean," he stated. "Weather permitting, I swim every morning."

"I don't know whether I'm a strong enough swimmer to overcome the waves and undertow," Rina admitted.

"Come with me tomorrow morning," Cleve suggested, turning off the local road and driving in the

direction of a billboard which boasted they were nearing
a restaurant that served the best seafood in Georgia.

"What time should I be ready?" she asked him.

"Six."

He maneuvered slowly over a portion of unpaved
road, then made a sharp right turn. A large, white-shingled farmhouse stood in the middle of a clearing,
surrounded by towering pine trees. It was early, yet the
restaurant's parking lot was crowded with cars.

Cleve pulled into one of the last spaces, turned off
the engine and smiled broadly at Rina. "Is six too early
for you?"

If it were she wouldn't admit it to him. "Not at all."

Rina waited as Cleve came around the car and
helped her out. His left arm went around her waist, and
his hand rested lightly on her hip as he led her up the
steps to the restaurant. His touch was impersonal, yet
protective. Again Rina found herself comparing his
touch to Jason's. Hadn't he said if she were his she would
never need another man? If she fell in love with Cleve
she would not want another man.

Mouth-watering smells wafted through the screen
door, along with seductive laughter and the sounds of a
tinkling piano playing a classic jazz composition.

Stained-glass windows, Tiffany lamps and
mahogany furnishings gave the restaurant a Victorian
ambience. Cleve did not drop his arm as they were
greeted by a tall, slender man with rimless glasses.

"Hey, Whit, I was wondering when you would show
up. Myles was by last week and said you had come…"

His words trailed off as his gaze shifted to Rina. "Welcome …"

"Rina Matthews," she supplied.

"Welcome, Miss Matthews," he continued smoothly. "I'm your host, Dewey Dixon, and I hope you find the food, music and atmosphere at The Crab Shack to your liking."

"I'm certain I will," she said with a friendly smile.

Dewey glanced at Cleve, then back at Rina. Cleve was not going to explain Rina. "Let me show you to your table."

It wasn't until after they were seated that Rina discovered The Crab Shack had been a Dixon family-owned business for more than fifty years and had established a reputation for concocting the best crab dishes along the coast. She also discovered the Whitneys had their own table at the restaurant. A reserved sign rested atop the table throughout the season when the Whitneys moved their summer residence to Whitney Hall.

Cleve picked up a menu and shifted closer to Rina, his trousered thigh pressing intimately against hers. "Do you drink anything stronger than milk and coffee?"

She blushed, and the golden light from a miniature Tiffany table lamp was complimentary to her smiling, shimmering mouth. "Wine."

"Good. Then order a bottle of champagne."

He ordered a bottle of Taittinger Comtes De Champagne without requesting the wine list, and Rina realized it was a wine Cleve had ordered many times before.

The position of the large booth permitted them a view of the room, while concealing them from the other diners.

A trio, consisting of a piano player, bassist and drummer, played pieces Rina had heard occasionally whenever her father put on classic 78s of John Coltrane, Charlie Parker and Miles Davis.

Cleve stared at her dreamy expression. "You like the music?"

She nodded. "It's nice."

"Better than classical?"

She recognized the teasing quality in his voice. "No."

"Maybe before the summer's over I can get you to change your mind."

Rina spread her fingers out on the stark white table-cloth. "I doubt that, Cleve."

He examined her beautifully tapered slender fingers. A network of pale blue veins showed under the golden skin covering her hands, He covered one of her hands with his, applying the slightest pressure when she tried pulling away.

"I think I'm going to change your mind about a lot of things, Rina."

Her head came up and she stared at him. Again, she encountered the expression he wore whenever his dark eyes impaled her with unwavering intensity. If she hadn't been as stubborn and independent as Cleveland

Whitney, she would have wilted under the lethal calmness of his stare.

Her breasts rose and fell heavily under the revealing neckline, and his gaze was drawn to her neck and chest, burning every spot it grazed.

"No," Rina's lips mumbled, while her heart said yes.

He leaned closer, his lids coming down and hiding his gaze from her. "Yes, Rina."

There was a bright flash of light, temporarily blinding both of them. Cleve sprang back and Rina blinked, trying to clear her vision.

Bright spots still danced before her eyes as she tried focusing on a tiny woman standing at the table with a camera dangling from a strap around her neck.

"Thank you, Mr. Whitney," the photographer crooned, then turned and walked away. Cleve's jaw hardened as he stared at her retreating back.

"Who was that?" Rina asked, holding tightly to his arm. She felt his muscles bunching up under her fingers. "Who is she, Cleve?"

He glanced down at Rina's hand, then slumped against the leather back of the booth.

"She's a photographer with a Savannah weekly."

She felt her pulse racing. The petite woman with a soft curling natural hairstyle had disappeared. "What is she going to do with that picture?"

"I don't know." Cleve let out his breath in an audible sigh.

Rina swallowed with difficulty. He didn't know, and she dreaded to think the worst. Would the photograph be used to create a scandal? Defame her reputation? And what about Cleve?

He dropped an arm around her shoulders, pulling her cheek to his solid shoulder. "Don't worry, Rina. There isn't much she can do with the photograph. So, you're safe."

I hope you're right, she prayed silently.

"My candidacy will become official this Saturday," Cleve informed her. "We'll begin with a high profile kick-off celebration at Whitney Hall."

Although she hadn't wanted to, somehow she knew she would be drawn into Cleveland Whitney's life.

And for the first time she wondered if securing the Whitney account had become more of a bust than a boon.

After several glasses of champagne and a platter of crab cakes, crabmeat étouffée and shrimp stuffed peppers shared with Cleve, Rina was too full and too relaxed to think about the photographer.

Cleve emptied the last of the champagne into her glass against her protests. "I can't drink anymore. I can't, Cleve," she insisted when he stared down at her.

"Would you like anything else to eat?"

She flashed a dreamy smile. "Where would I put it?"

He touched a spot behind her ear, his finger lingering over the tiny gold stud in her pierced lobe. "Right here," he said in a husky tone.

She couldn't stop the shudder wracking her body at his light touch. His lips replaced his finger and Rina moaned inwardly. Didn't he realize what he was doing to her? Her hands curled into tight fists on her lap. And within the second it took for his mouth to taste her flesh, she knew what she had wanted from the moment she saw Cleveland Whitney. She wanted him; she not only wanted his touch, his kiss, but all of him.

Levelheaded, conservative Rina Matthews wanted a man she had known for only one day. What was the matter with her? She wasn't looking for a fling before she committed herself to Jason…

The thought of Jason broke the sensual spell Cleve had woven, and she pulled away from his questing mouth. "No, Cleve," she gasped. Even to herself she sounded weak and ineffective.

Cleve took in her parted lips and glazed stare. He didn't believe her weak protest. "Is it really no, Rina?"

"Of course it's no," she retorted with a return of confidence and renewed spirit. "I'm…"

"I know. Practically engaged," he finished for her.

That wasn't what she was going to say, but she let him think it was. He signaled for the waiter and signed the check. He nodded in acknowledgment when Rina thanked him for dinner.

Both of them were lost in their own private thoughts on the return trip to Whitney Hall, and Rina was surprised when Cleve followed her up the staircase to her room.

"I always make certain a lady returns home safely after a date," he explained, smiling down at her.

She braced her back against the door, raising a delicate eyebrow. "I didn't realize it was a date."

He chuckled softly. "There's a great deal you don't realize, Rina. It was a date," he confirmed.

"Thank you for an enjoyable evening." She extended her hand.

He ignored her hand, leaning over and pressing a light kiss to her forehead. "You're welcome, Rina. I'll come for you at six."

"I'll be ready," she said in a breathless tone. The heat and smell of his masculine body left her trembling with a foreign yearning.

Cleve turned but stopped as Abigail came down the hallway, a frown creasing her smooth forehead. "How was your outing with Em-Jay, Mother?"

"Wonderful," Abigail replied quickly. Her gaze darted from Rina to Cleve. "But it's hours past Emily-Jane's bedtime and she won't go to sleep. You know how hyper she gets when she doesn't have enough sleep."

"Have you read her a story?" Cleve asked his mother.

"I tried." Abigail glanced at Rina. "She wants Rina to read to her."

Cleve studied Rina intently, his gaze impassive. "Oh, I see," he murmured.

And so did Rina when she said, "Cleve can read to her."

"She doesn't want Cleveland to read to her," Abigail insisted. "She wants you to read to her."

Rina felt Cleve's resentment, strong and threatening. She managed a small smile for Abigail. "If the child needs her sleep I'd better get this over with quickly."

Brushing past Cleve, she headed down the hallway and down the stairs to Emily-Jane's bedroom.

Walking into the child's room, Rina found Emily-Jane standing up on her bed, tossing the stuffed rabbit up in the air. The little girl let out an excited yelp when she saw Rina.

"Are you going to read to me?"

She sat down on the bed, pulling Emily-Jane down beside her. "Yes. But you must promise me that you'll let your uncle Cleve read to you tomorrow."

"I don't like him reading to me," Emily-Jane whined, pushing out her lower lip. She crawled onto Rina's lap and looped her arms around her neck. "He doesn't make it fun like you do."

She cradled the child to her chest and kissed her forehead. "You must think about his feelings, Emily-Jane."

"He can feel any way he wants," Emily-Jane insisted stubbornly.

Rina decided on another approach. "Do you love your uncle, Emily-Jane?"

Emily-Jane looked up at Rina, her eyes dark and serious. "Yes. Uncle Cleve is like my second daddy."

"Then you know how much he loves you." Emily-Jane nodded, then pushed her thumb into her mouth. "When someone loves us very much we sometimes do or say things that hurt that person without our being aware that we're doing it."

"I hurt Uncle Cleve?"

"You've hurt his feelings, Emily-Jane. Cleve is the person who usually reads to you when you go to bed, and now you don't want him to read to you because I'm here."

"Is he crying?"

She tried not to laugh. "No, he isn't crying. But I'm certain he feels lonely because you don't want him to read to you."

"He can read to me."

"When?"

Emily-Jane removed her thumb, cocking her head to one side. She sucked in her breath, her narrow shoulders dropping. "I don't know. I have to think about it."

She gently pushed the little girl from her lap, settling her on the bed. Pulling a sheet up over her colorful pajamas, she said sternly, "You think about this, young lady. I'll read to you tonight, but not tomorrow. Cleve and I are going to take turns reading to you. if I read tonight, then Cleve will read tomorrow."

Emily-Jane's lower lip trembled. "I don't want him to read to me tomorrow."

Rina stood up. "I'm sorry, Emily-Jane. Then I can't read to you tonight."

"Don't go!" Emily-Jane sat up quickly. Her mouth settled into a pout. "Okay. Uncle Cleve can read to me tomorrow."

She moved over to the chair beside the bed and selected a book. She didn't think she was going to win the battle of wills with the child. At three and a half, Emily-Jane Whitney Jackson had exhibited the willfulness she had inherited from her maternal grandfather and uncle.

She glanced up after two minutes and found Emily-Jane clutching the rabbit to her chest, thumb in mouth and asleep. Rina closed the book and returned it to the bedside table. At the last moment she kissed the girl's cheek, then turned off the lamp.

Rina stood staring down at Emily-Jane, remembering her own episodes of rebellious behavior when her father remarried.

She had refused to understand Gabriel's need for permanent companionship when Evelyn moved into the house as his wife and her stepmother.

She had addressed Evelyn as she or her and refused to answer when spoken to. All things changed when Evelyn became pregnant with Scott. Evelyn's nausea was evident throughout her confinement, and there were times when Rina thought her new stepmother was going to die.

She had lost her mother, and she feared that she was going to lose her stepmother too. Somewhere among her childish fears Rina knew Gabriel would never survive the loss of another wife, so she began helping Evelyn every chance she got.

Woman and child became very close, and when the tiny infant boy was born, Evelyn gave Rina the honor of naming him.

Gabriel and Evelyn never knew that Rina had developed a crush on a boy in one of her classes whose name was Scott. At twelve, Rina had been too shy to reveal her newly awakening interest in the opposite sex.

But now at twenty-nine was she any different than she was at twelve?

Not much, she thought, because the emotions coursing through her head and body betrayed her every time she saw or thought about Cleveland Whitney.

Cleve, just being who he was, had unknowingly broken down barriers Rina had erected around her to protect herself from *affaires de coeur*. Jason on occasion complained that she was too serious and unresponsive, but what Jason did not know was that she feared loving and losing a part of herself when it was over. She knew Jason well enough to know he could walk away from their relationship almost unscathed, while she would be the one left with the emotional scars.

A nightlight glimmered dimly in Emily-Jane's bedroom as Rina walked out and closed the door. She made it back to her own bedroom without encountering Abigail or Cleve.

She undressed, washed her face, unpinned her hair and slipped into bed. Like Emily-Jane, she was asleep within minutes. And this night there were no sensual fantasies to arouse her from her deep slumber.

CHAPTER 8

"I'm coming," Rina called out at the incessant tapping on her bedroom door. She took a quick glance at the clock on the mantel. It was only five forty-five. Opening the door, she glared up at a startled Cleve. "You're early. Is something wrong?" she asked, as he stood staring down at her, his gaze moving leisurely over the wealth of unbound hair flowing around her bare shoulders.

The modest black maillot clinging to her body accentuated rather than detracted from her slender feminine curves. The legs were cut higher than Rina would have preferred, but the suit covered more than most of the other suits she had tried on when she decided she needed new swimwear.

"I—I'm sorry, Rina. I thought that…that…"

"What's the matter, Cleve?" She could not imagine what had startled the formidable district attorney so much that he was at a loss for words. "Come in." Stepping back, she motioned for him to enter her bedroom.

"No…no. I'll wait out here. I just thought we would start early, then share breakfast before you begin working this morning," he explained, finally putting his words together without stuttering.

Rina shrugged her shoulders, then walked over to the armoire and pulled a T-shirt from one of the drawers. The oversized shirt was the perfect cover-up. It ended an inch above her knees. She pushed her bare feet into a pair of old running shoes and tied them up.

"Bring a change of clothes," Cleve ordered from the hall.

She stuck her head outside the door and found Cleve with his back pressed against the wall. "Why?"

He pushed his hands into the pockets of a pair of shorts. "You can shower and change at my place instead of coming back here. It'll save you some time."

Perhaps it was the early hour, but Cleve wasn't making sense to Rina. "Don't you live here?"

"Yes and no."

She folded her hands on her hips. "Talk to me, Cleveland Whitney."

"Get your things together and I'll explain." He pushed away from the wall.

"I won't do anything until you tell me what's going on," she countered. Rina's stubbornness had surfaced.

"Damn mule-headed female," he muttered under his breath.

"You're wasting precious time." Cleve glared at Rina and, when she didn't move, he shook his head. "All right! I have a room here, but I also have a house down by the beach," he practically shouted.

"Now, darling, was that so difficult?" she crooned, grinning broadly.

"Go, Rina. You're testing my one last very ragged nerve."

She ducked back into the bedroom, Cleve's smothered laughter following her. She was aware that she tested him; what she did not know was that she had tested him the way no other woman had and bested him every time.

"I'm ready," she announced as she walked out of the room with a nylon backpack. "And it's six o'clock."

Cleve reached for her hand, holding it in a firm grip. "One of these days you're going to push me a little too far, Rina."

"You're wasting time, Cleve," she flung back at him.

His fingers tightened on hers as he led her down the hallway and down the flight of curving stairs. "Now follow me," he said, leading her through the kitchen to a door off the pantry.

He released her hand long enough to pick up a large lantern. Seconds later her fingers were back in his strong protective grasp as he opened the door and descended a flight of stairs.

"Stay close to me, Rina."

She had no choice but to follow him through what she thought of as a tunnel. It was about six feet wide and six feet in height. Cleve had to bend his head and shoulders as he led the way through the cool, damp passage. The hard packed ground was smooth under her feet. She quickened her steps to keep up with his longer legs.

Rina tried seeing beyond the strong beam of the lantern, but encountered total darkness. "Where are we going?"

"To my house."

"How far is it from here?"

"Only a quarter of a mile through the tunnel. It would be twice that if you went above ground."

She followed him blindly through the darkness, praying the batteries in the lantern would last. "I know every inch of this tunnel without a light," Cleve said, almost reading her mind. "My brothers and I used to play down here all the time when we were kids. Sometimes we played tricks on one another and hid the flashlight. I always found my way out because I memorized the different markings along the tunnel wall."

There was only the sound of their breathing and the crunch of dirt beneath the soles of their shoes. Rina had heard about doors that led to secret passages in old houses but never thought she would experience it firsthand. Cleve slowed, then stopped. He flicked off the lantern, plunging them into blackness.

Her slight cry of surprise echoed loudly. "Don't move, sweetheart," Cleve warned quietly.

She was too frightened to register the endearment as she moved closer to Cleve, looping both arms around his waist. "Stop playing games, Cleve," she gasped, pressing her face to his chest.

Cleve raised his left arm and pressed the heel of his hand against a jutting piece of rock. A section of the wall swung open, revealing a staircase. A shaft of light from above filtered downward.

"You can let me go now," he said softly to Rina, certain that her fingernails had left small half-moon impressions in his flesh under his T-shirt.

Rina smoothed out the wrinkled fabric covering his back. "I'm sorry."

Cleve lowered his head and pressed a light kiss on the end of her nose. "It's all right." He urged her forward. "You can go up first. Be careful because the steps are usually quite slippery."

Fingers touching cold stone, she climbed slowly up the moist steps. First there was near-darkness, then bright light the moment she stepped into Cleve's house, blinking.

Track lights, walls covered with white planking and a towering loft with a beamed ceiling had turned the expansive space into functional living quarters.

If Whitney Hall was a historic landmark, then Cleve's house was a modern masterpiece. The white walls were lined with framed impressionist art, a sophisticated entertainment system and row upon row of books.

There were no walls separating the living room from the kitchen and dining areas. Everything was displayed in panoramic dimensions: dark green leather pieces of furniture were arranged throughout for lounging; beveled glass and brass tables, cane chairs, imported Floco oyster-white area rugs, towering potted cacti, and a magnificent white concert grand piano set the stage for living and dining.

A floating stairway with bleached pine steps and a brass banister curved upward to what Rina knew were the sleeping quarters.

Her gaping mouth revealed her surprise. Shaking her head in amazement, she whispered, "It's wonderful, Cleve. I take that back. It's exquisite!"

And it was. The front of the house was a wall of glass facing the beach. Ribbons of bright sunlight glinted off the white wood walls, white rugs and piano like shimmering silver streamers.

Rina walked slowly over to the wall of glass and stared out at the line of endless water merging with the sky. She felt the power of the ocean with its hypnotic, invisible pull and took a backward step.

"Awesome, isn't it?" Cleve asked against her ear.

She shivered, nodding. The sensations wracking her body were as much from Cleve moving silently to stand close, too close, to her as they were from marveling at the beauty of her surroundings.

Looking at the blue sky with puffy white clouds, the pristine wind-blown sand and the rising and cresting of the blue-gray water, Rina wondered how long had it been since she had taken the time to enjoy the miracle of Nature.

"This is the first summer in a very long time that I've been able to enjoy it," Cleve replied, as if reading her mind. He rested both hands on her shoulders. "It feels good to get off the bureaucratic merry-go-round and put both feet on solid ground."

Rina wanted to melt against his solid body, but quelled the reckless urge. "What about your election bid, Cleve?"

"What about it, Rina?"

She shivered again. His soft voice, his warmth and the strength of his long fingers stirred secret desires she had successfully repressed for years. Pulling away from his loose hold, she turned and stared up at his solemn expression. His eyes were darker than usual and filled with an emotion she couldn't read.

"Won't you have to spend a lot of time away from here when you begin campaigning in Savannah?"

He offered her a slow smile. "Not until early August. And that will allow me at least two months to enjoy my home before voters tire of seeing my face or listening to all of the election rhetoric they've heard before."

His gaze moved leisurely over her face and his smile widened. "I have a feeling this summer is going to be a memorable one. A memorable one indeed, Rina Matthews."

His eyes blazed down into hers, revealing what she already knew. Walking into Whitney Hall and meeting Cleveland Whitney had changed her, changed her forever.

Rina had no way of knowing that Cleveland Whitney was not the same man he had been before meeting her.

"I wish you luck, Cleve," she said in a quiet tone.

"I have all of the luck I'll ever need," he countered in a voice as quiet as Rina's. "Being a Whitney affords me everything I'll ever need. However, being a Whitney does not always give me what I want, Rina," he stated emphatically between clenched teeth.

Again, she was mesmerized by the unmoving, unblinking Cleveland Whitney. Her whole being seemed to be filled with a waiting; a waiting for him to make the first move; a waiting for him to make it easy for her to acknowledge her growing attraction to him; a waiting for him to make it easy for her to face the harsh reality that Jason was not the man with whom she truly wanted to spend the rest of her life.

She felt a rush of guilt at her traitorous thoughts. She loved Jason. Jason Harper was handsome and exciting, but he didn't excite her.

I'm only attracted to Cleveland Whitney because of his reputation, she rationalized. *It's the Whitney name.*

"Let's go swimming," Rina suggested, breaking the mood and spell that had held the both of them captive.

Dropping her backpack, she wagged her fingers at a stunned Cleve. "Come, darling, you're wasting precious time, again."

She kicked off her shoes and pulled the T-shirt over her head, and before Cleve could undo the waistband of his shorts, Rina slid back the glass doors and raced across the beach to the water's edge. She had almost made it to the water when she heard his footsteps.

The early morning sun was hot on her back, yet not hot enough to offset the icy waters of the Atlantic Ocean. The surf lapped around her legs and feet as she waded slowly into the water.

"Ninny," Cleve taunted, coming up behind her.

Without warning, he hoisted her effortlessly over his shoulder and carried her out where waves crashed against his chest.

Rina pounded his bare, muscled back with her fists. "Put me down, Cleve!"

He took several steps, then complied, dropping her. Her toes struggled to touch something solid, but when they didn't she knew she had to tread water or sink.

She opened her mouth to scream at him, but Cleve couldn't hear her. He was swimming strongly out into the ocean, and she watched in awe as his body cut the surface of the water like a sleek eel.

Rina soon forgot about the initial sting of the cold water and began swimming after him.

They swam, floated and raced each other until they both tired.

"I'm ready to go back," she shouted, her chest rising and falling heavily after the strenuous exertion.

Cleve swam to her side, his face looming above hers, blocking out the rays of the sun. Droplets of water clung to his face and smooth chest like multi-faceted diamonds on dark brown silk.

"Tired, sweetheart?"

Rina nodded, trying to conserve her strength. She also did not trust her response to his calling her sweetheart. It was the second time that morning he had called her that. The first was when she had been frightened in the tunnel after he turned off the lantern.

He caught her upper body in a grip lifeguards used when saving drowning victims and swam strongly back to the beach.

Gathering her in his arms, he carried her around to the back of the house and settled her onto a webbed lounge on an outdoor patio under a green and white striped awning.

"Do you think you'll need mouth-to-mouth?" he teased, leaning over her prone body.

Rina waved a delicate hand, closing her eyes. "Go away, Cleveland." Her soft mouth was smiling.

He ignored her protest, pressing a light kiss on her chilled lips, warming not only her mouth but her entire body.

"I'll be back with breakfast in a few minutes," he promised, staring down into her startled gaze.

Rina was too shocked to respond. She stared at his broad back until he disappeared into the house, and it was only then that her trembling began. She reached for a leaf-green towel on a side table and rubbed her arms and legs until her flesh was no longer cold but hot and tingling.

Cleve returned with a tray of freshly squeezed orange juice, fresh melon balls, hot fluffy biscuits and a half dozen little crystal jars filled with jellies and preserves which he placed on a wicker serving cart. Quickly and expertly he set a round wicker table with a dark green linen tablecloth, napkins, china and silver.

She forced her gaze away from his near-nude body. Cleve hadn't bothered to put his shorts back on over his swim trunks and there were times when she couldn't stop her eyes from lingering on his solid thighs and muscled legs.

Cleve walked over to her, extending a hand. "Breakfast is ready," he announced, smiling and bowing slightly from the waist.

Rina offered her hand, and he pulled her up from the lounge in one smooth motion, then seated her at the table. He spread a matching green linen napkin over her bare knees before taking his own seat opposite her.

She picked up a biscuit and filled its fluffy middle with a liberal amount of strawberry preserves from a small silver spoon. Taking a bite, Rina slowly savored the taste of plump strawberries.

She smiled across the table at her dining partner. "This is truly living. An early morning swim in the ocean and breakfast al fresco."

Cleve picked up a large crystal goblet filled with orange juice. "I'll take credit for the locale, but not for the meal. Mrs. Bailey prepared breakfast."

Rina took a sip of her own freshly squeezed juice. "A most winning combination."

He shifted a dark eyebrow. "How's that?"

"Mrs. Bailey's cooking, your house and your company," she replied, lowering her glass.

His eyes never left her face. "Thank you, Rina. But you must have dinner here. There are times when I sit here for hours and watch nature prepare for nightfall. It can be quite humbling."

She noted the faraway look in his eyes. "It must have been fascinating growing up here."

He nodded. "It was. We spent all of our summers at Whitney Hall and some of the holidays when the entire family decided to get together." He hesitated, a smile creasing his face. "Christmas at Whitney Hall is always a special event."

Christmas was also special to Rina. Her birthday was December 25th.

"When did you discover the tunnel under the house?" she asked.

"I was told about it as a child," he replied. "It served as a storage cellar when the main house was first constructed, but abandoned years later when a smoke and ice-house were built above ground. Subsequent owners of the property were unaware that it had become an escape route for runaway slaves. This house was once a warehouse, and many of the slaves hid out in the loft with bales of cotton, rice and indigo, sometimes waiting weeks before a ship would drop anchor and send a dinghy to the beach to pick up the luckier ones who sailed northward to freedom."

"Did Noah Whitney know about the tunnel?"

Cleve studied Rina thoughtfully for a moment. It was apparent she was familiar with his family's history. "Yes."

She leaned forward. "If he lived on the plantation and knew about the tunnel, why didn't he run away?"

He smiled at her. "Noah was a freeman of color. He lived here quite comfortably as a skilled blacksmith and carpenter. And Noah had saved enough money that after the Civil War ended he bought Whitney Hall for back taxes. The name on the deed merely changed from Jacob Elias Whitney, retired colonel of the Confederate States of America, to Noah Whitney, who had purchased his freedom from the former ten years before."

Her luminous eyes sparkled with interest. A rising breeze stirred curls that were drying over her forehead. "Was Noah active in the underground railroad?"

Cleve managed a half-smile. "Noah played his part as a courier. No one suspected him because after he'd purchased his freedom most people expected him to go north. But he stayed and helped dozens slip away."

Rina shivered slightly, trying to imagine the indescribable joy the slaves must have felt when they attained their freedom.

"Don't you find it eerie to live on property that has been in the same family for hundreds of years, reliving their history and secrets generation after generation?"

Cleve pursed his lips, smiling. "It is," he agreed. "But records indicate this land has always belonged to a Whitney, white or black."

"Has anyone written a book about the Whitneys?"

Leaning forward, he rested his chin on the heel of his left hand. "Are you volunteering?"

She laughed lightly. "I'm an accountant, not an aspiring author."

His gaze moved down to the soft swell of breasts pushing against the bodice of her swimsuit. "What made you decide to become an accountant?"

She shrugged narrow shoulders. "It was either accounting or archaeology."

"Why not archaeology?"

"I changed my mind when I realized I would not always have the comfort of a warm shower or clean fingernails." She visually examined her tapered manicured fingernails.

He stabbed at a ball of honeydew melon with his fork. "Was that the only reason?"

Her expression mirrored seriousness. "It was reason enough for me. Why did you become an attorney?"

"Perry Mason," he mumbled softly under his breath.

She leaned over the table. "Perry Mason?"

"I liked Perry Mason," Cleve said defensively.

Rina's eyes crinkled in amusement. She couldn't stop the laughter from bubbling upward as her shoulders shook. "That excuse is even weaker than mine."

"No, it's not," he retorted. "At least I didn't choose a career based on vanity," he added, pouting.

"What do you call it, Cleveland Whitney? Perry Mason is a fictional character who can't lose a case because it's written that way from the beginning." She giggled when she noted his crestfallen expression. "I'm sorry, Cleve," she gasped as he rose threateningly from his chair. "I'm sorry! No!" she screamed when he quickly moved and pulled her from her chair.

Tears were streaming down her face as Cleve tickled her relentlessly; she was hiccupping weakly when his arms tightened around her waist, holding her captive.

Rina held onto his neck, her breasts flattening against his bare chest. She felt the slow, steady beating of his heart keeping tempo with her own. His touching her, cradling her to his body, filling her with his strength and warmth, and drawing her into himself made her aware that the teasing had evaporated quickly.

Her head fell forward, a curtain of hair sweeping his neck. His hold lessened slightly, permitting her to slide down his body, Cleve's breast branding hers through the spandex of the maillot. The involuntary tremors of arousal began in the area between her thighs and spread outwardly, drugging her body and her senses.

Cleve's breathing quickened, his fingers tightening painfully on her tiny waist. He held her suspended effortlessly in the air, an invisible force bonding them together.

He finally released her, and Rina sank back down to the safety of her chair. Pulling her knees to her chest, she wound her arms around her legs.

"Rina?"

She ignored Cleve's husky entreaty, closing her eyes.

"Rina, look at me." Cleve squatted down in front of her. Her head came up, and he recognized the tormented anguish in her hazel eyes. "I'm not going to lie and say I'm not attracted to you," he admitted. "But also, I'm never take from you what you're not willing to give me."

She was torn by conflicting emotions. She didn't know what she wanted to give him; it couldn't be love because she loved another man. Or did she?

"All I can offer you is my friendship, Cleve," she replied, her even tone masking anxiety. "Nothing more."

Rina prayed she would discover what it was about Cleveland Whitney that drew her to him, made her desire him with an urgency she had never felt with Jason, or with any other man.

Cleve stared back at her, only the throbbing muscle in his lean jaw revealing his own uneasiness. Was he also feeling what she was feeling? Did he know what he wanted from her?

They had progressed beyond a verbal sparring, a distrust of one another. Both of them had been stripped bare, leaving only a man and a woman with emotions that were strong and unchecked.

Lowering his gaze, he said quietly, "If that's all you're offering, then I'll accept it." He stood and she rose with him.

"Please excuse me. I have to get dressed." She felt his gaze on her stiff spine as she turned and walked back into the house.

Rina knew she had made a mistake. The moment Cleve held her she had lowered her defenses; she had let him in and he had known of her surrender.

She picked up her backpack and discarded T-shirt and found the downstairs bathroom.

It won't happen again, she thought, stripping off her swimsuit and stepping into a shower stall. She showered and shampooed her hair, repeating the promise to herself over and over.

And when she walked out of the bathroom dressed in a loose-fitting linen sundress in a soft peach color with a pair of leather Italian sandals of the same shade, she was confident she would keep her promise.

CHAPTER 9

Rina spent the morning going through six months of bank reconciliation statements for Abigail's household accounts. Whitney Hall's historic landmark status required maintenance of separate accounting expenses.

She detailed expenses for Abigail's personal Savannah residence, noting the mounting figures in the contribution column. There was no doubting the Whitney matriarch's overwhelming generosity for two of her favorite charities.

The phone rang in the stillness of the room, permitting her a much-needed break.

She picked up the receiver. "Rina Matthews."

"Rina. Bill Newton."

She would have recognized the distinctive gravelly voice even if Bill hadn't bothered to identify himself. "How are you, Bill?" There was a pause before Bill spoke again.

"I think I'm a lot better than you are right now."

She flinched at the tone of his voice. "What's the matter?"

"Damn, I hate making these calls, Rina."

She clamped her teeth together. There had to be a very good reason why the manager of the bank where she had her personal and business accounts was calling her across the state.

"I have checks drawn on Harper and Matthews I can't pay." The words tumbled quickly from the bank manager's mouth.

Her body stiffened in shock. "What!" Her voice was barely a whisper.

"We paid a check yesterday Harper had signed over to some automobile leasing concern."

Rina searched her mind for a meaning behind the words coming from the bank manager. What leasing company? On what car?

Fear and anger knotted inside of her, but she forced herself to remain calm. "Bill, please tell me what is going on."

She listened, not interrupting, as each breath she drew seemed to solidify in her throat. Within minutes it was clear. Bill had done the right thing to call her.

"What do you want me to do, Rina?"

"What checks have come in?" Bill read off the check amounts and the payees. They were the checks she had written before she left Atlanta. "Don't return them," she ordered.

"But, Rina…"

"I'll cover them, Bill."

"With what funds, Rina? You'll exceed your line of credit."

"Tomorrow I'll drive to Savannah and transfer money from my personal account."

"Are you certain you want to do that?"

She closed her eyes. "I have no choice." She had to cover checks for rental space for the office and make certain there were enough monies for the upcoming weekly payroll.

"Anything else, Rina?"

She opened her eyes, biting down hard on her lower lip until it throbbed like a pulse. "Yes, there is. I want you to call me before you pay any check from the Harper and Matthews account with Jason's signature. And I mean any check."

"Now, Rina, what if Harper…"

"I'll take care of my partner, thank you."

There was a loud sigh from the other end of the telephone wire. "You've got it. I'll flag the account, so if I'm not here someone else will follow through."

She managed a strained grimace. "Thanks, Bill."

She hung up and her fingers curled into tight fists. Fingernails bit painfully into the soft flesh of her palms.

Counting slowly to ten, she picked up the telephone receiver, dialing. She had to remain in control.

There was a break in the connection after the second ring. "Good afternoon. Harper and Matthews."

"Aimee, this is Rina. Put me through to Jason."

"He's not here, Rina."

"Where is he!" She caught herself. She was screaming at the receptionist when it was Jason she wanted to scream at.

"I'm sorry, Aimee," she apologized, "but do you know where he is?"

"His appointment book has lunch with, wait a minute I can't read his handwriting. The name looks like Garritson. Oh, yes, it's Thomas Garritson."

The Garritson account was one Jason had been courting for months and still had not secured.

"Did he indicate where they were eating lunch?"

"Probably out at the Garritson place," Aimee volunteered. "He had me call the florist to have flowers sent out there this morning," the receptionist continued: "He ordered six dozen long-stem red roses for Mrs. Garritson's daughter. Tiffany."

Rina's left hand squeezed the telephone receiver in a death-grip while the fingers of her right hand drummed on the desktop.

"Aimee," she began slowly, "I want you to listen to everything I'm going to tell you. If you have to, write it down. I want you to call Mr. Garritson's house and tell Jason Edward Harper to call me back at Whitney Hall. If you can't reach him there, then I want you to call Jason Edward Harper's house and leave the same message on his answering machine. But if he returns to the office before you go home, then you can tell him in person."

"I've got it, Rina."

"Good." Rina smiled for the first time since receiving the call from Bill Newton.

She hung up and beat a staccato rhythm on the desk. She couldn't be in two places simultaneously; she couldn't audit Abigail's finances and take care of her own business too.

Covering her face with her hands, she mentally willed the tension to go away. She had tried understanding Jason, his moods which changed like quicksilver, his aspirations and his driving need for recognition.

And she had also overlooked many things Jason did that she found unacceptable or inappropriate. She had covered for him, made excuses for him to her parents, and she had told herself that she loved him.

But at that moment Rina felt more loathing for Jason Harper than she did loving. Everything about the man bothered her from his casual approach to managing the office to his preoccupation with the selling of Jason Edward Harper. His marketing plan was not for the firm, but for himself. And she knew he was not going to change, which meant she had to change.

She worked through lunch, refusing Abigail's offer to join her and Emily-Jane. She begged off with the excuse that she was awaiting a call from Jason, but the call never came. What had been red-hot anger turned into a slow seething, and now she was not certain how she would react to hearing Jason's voice or his explanation for overdrawing their business account.

She was devoid of any emotion as she made her way to her bedroom to change for dinner. All of her movements were stiff and mechanical as she showered and dressed, and when she walked into the dining room, she had schooled her features not to reveal the inner torment pressing down on her mind and body like weighted steel.

Cleve rose from his position at the table, heading toward her. His dark eyes moved slowly over her delicate features. Lowering his chin, he smiled down at her, and surprisingly Rina returned his smile.

"It's only the two of us again," he said softly.

Her gaze shifted to the table, and it was only then that she realized the dining room table had not been set for dining.

"Mother and Em-Jay decided they both wanted to eat out," Cleve explained.

"And what is it you want, Cleve?" she asked.

Rina did not know why she had asked him that, but she had to know if he wanted her the way she wanted him.

Slowly and deliberately Cleve's gaze dropped from Rina's face to her shoulders and down to her breasts.

She felt the heat from his seductive perusal, and from her own body's traitorous reaction to his commanding virility.

"I want you…" Cleve was charmed by the rush of dark color flushing her suntanned golden-brown cheeks, "to share dinner with me at my place," he completed, as her eyes widened in apparent surprise.

Rina wanted to run, run as far away from Whitney Hall as she could. But she knew that wasn't possible. Escaping Whitney Hall and Cleveland Whitney would not permit her to escape from herself. Her instinctive response to him was so powerful, so intense, that she had tried and failed to understand what it was about the man that made her so reckless.

And she knew he had been right. If she belonged to Cleveland Whitney she would never need another man.

Peering up at him through her lashes, she gave him a sensual smile. "Are you cooking tonight?"

Cleve reached for her left hand, threading his fingers through hers. "Yes, ma'am."

"I'm not going through the tunnel," Rina warned as Cleve led her from the dining room. He tightened his grip on her fingers. "I'll carry you."

"Forget it, Cleve."

"Don't be a ninny, Rina," he taunted again.

She pulled back, forcing him to stop. "I'll be anything I want to be, Cleveland Whitney. But I'm not going through that tunnel this night?"

Cleve stared down at her, his eyes brimming with understanding and tenderness. "Does the tunnel frighten you, sweetheart?"

She closed her eyes against his intense gaze. *You frighten me, Cleve,* she thought. *And I frighten myself.*

In one forward motion, Rina was in Cleve's arms, her soft curves molded to the contours of his hard body.

"Cleve." She couldn't keep the tremor from her voice.

"It's all right, sweetheart," he crooned, his breath hot and moist against her ear.

Rina felt no desire to pull out of his protective embrace. He was warm, comforting, and she felt a slow, building desire she had never felt with Jason.

Why couldn't he be Jason Harper, her head screamed silently. Why couldn't Cleve be her business partner and the man she planned to marry?

Why? Why? The whys attacked her relentlessly. "I don't mind walking to your place," she said, tilting her head back to look up at his lean, dark-skinned face.

She visually admired the rich mahogany undertones in his brown skin, the thick black silkiness of his arching eyebrows and the inky darkness of his close-cut, tightly curled hair.

She wanted to run her fingers over the smooth, firm flesh of his shaven jaw and outline the sensual curve of his full mouth. She wanted to commit every plane and hollow of his face to memory.

"We'll drive down and walk back," he suggested, smiling and dropping a kiss on the end of her nose.

Her body stiffened and he released her; the magical spell was broken. The feel of his mouth on her nose jolted Rina back to reality. He was treating her as if she were his little sister, not as a woman who lusted after him. And that was what she felt for Cleveland Whitney, lust.

But hadn't he said he was only going to take what she was willing to offer him? And hadn't she said that could only be friendship? And that was how Cleveland Whitney was treating her, like a friend.

"I don't mind walking there and back," she insisted.

Cleve glanced down at her low-heeled shoes and nodded. Hand-in-hand he led her out of the house. They walked in silence past the fragrant white roses, flowering fruit trees, boxwood gardens and across the meadow filled with a riot of wildflowers.

Walking through the meadow reminded Rina of her erotic dream and the elusive stranger who had chased her. She shivered and Cleve registered the slight shudder.

"Are you cold?" he questioned incredulously. The nighttime temperatures were still in the low eighties.

A wave of heat followed her shiver. "No, not at all." She was comfortably dressed in a pair of black linen slacks with a black and white jungle print blouse.

"What's on the menu tonight?" she asked after another lengthy silence.

"I thought I'd grill some steaks and throw a salad together."

Rina found Cleve to be an excellent cook. The steaks were cooked to succulent perfection on a gas grill, and he prepared accompanying side dishes of grilled vegetables, tiny cubes of roasted white potatoes and herbed, fresh tomato salad with mozzarella cheese, sprinkled with olive oil.

She was more than content to sit out under the stars and watch the sun sink beyond the line of the ocean. It was exactly as Cleve had boasted; the sight was awesome and humbling.

Cleve refused to let her assist him in preparing dinner but acquiesced when she offered to help him clean up.

She hummed to herself as she dried dishes, handing them to Cleve to put away in overhead cabinets, missing his surreptitious glances. He was fully aware of the domestic scene they presented. He was totally unaware that it was a situation that Rina could quite easily get used to.

The return to Whitney Hall was slower as Cleve held her waist instead of her hand, helping her over uneven portions of the vast property. She thanked him for dinner before he escorted her up the stairs, pressing a kiss to his smooth cheek.

"Good night, Cleve."

"Good night, Rina." He stood at the foot of the staircase, watching her ascend until she disappeared from sight.

Moonlight silvered every surface in the bedroom as Rina lay on the bed listening to the soft sounds of her own breathing. Sleep was elusive again.

A strange restlessness assailed her and for the first time in years she felt helpless. She felt used up, burned out.

She had pushed herself for more than a year without taking a break. When was she going to get off her own merry-go-round and enjoy life?

She slipped out of bed and walked over to the French doors. Opening the doors, she stepped out onto the veranda. A whisper of a breeze lifted the diaphanous cotton batiste nightgown before molding it to the slender curves of her body.

Raising her arms, she reveled in the coolness sweeping over her face and bare arms. The tangy smell of the ocean filled her nostrils, clearing her head.

The night was clear, refreshing and healing. Living at Whitney Hall was relaxing and healing. Sharing dinner at Cleve's house had been enjoyable and healing.

Closing her eyes, she whispered, "I could stay here forever."

"Is that really what you want, Rina? To stay here forever?"

Her eyes opened and she stared at Cleve. He stood less than five feet from her. How long had he been there? Why hadn't she heard his approach?

Suddenly she was aware of her revealing nightgown. She crossed her arms over her chest in a protective gesture.

"What are you doing here?"

Cleve closed the distance between them, his tall figure looming powerfully in the moonlight. "I live here, Rina."

She tried to make out his expression in the shadows. "I know you live here, but…"

His fingers curled around her wrists, bringing her arms down. "There's no need to hide from me," he said quietly. "Your swimsuit revealed a lot more flesh than this…garment."

His forefinger pushed a narrow strap up on her shoulder, then grazed the gold chain around her neck before toying with the tiny locket suspended from the chain and nestled between her breasts.

But they had been equals earlier that morning. His brief swim trunks were not what she thought of as modest. They rode low on his slim hips, leaving nothing to her imagination as to his obvious maleness. The sparse triangle of spandex teased more than it concealed.

Her heart pumped wildly under her breasts. "I didn't expect to find you lurking outside my bedroom."

Cleve released her, leaning back against the wrought-iron railing. The moonlight highlighted her face and silhouetted her body. "That can't be helped. We share this veranda. My bedroom is next to yours."

"Then it was you!" Rina exclaimed.

Cleve's eyebrows shifted. "Me what?" he questioned innocently.

She hesitated. What if she were wrong? What if Cleve hadn't left the roses?

"The roses," she said, hoping she was correct in assuming Cleve was her mystery visitor.

"Did you like them?" His voice held a hint of laughter as he crossed his arms over his chest.

She saw a flash of white teeth in the darkness. "Yes. Very much. Thank you," she added in a husky tone.

Cleve turned, bracing his forearms on the top of the railing. "I wanted to apologize to you, Rina, but I didn't know how." He stared out into the blackness of the night. "Because of Harper's threat I'd prematurely tried you and found you guilty of being a thief."

Rina felt a surge of relief flow through her. Cleve did trust her. It had happened without her having to prove to him that she had no intention of misappropriating his mother's fortune.

"I have to think about your apology," she drawled, filled with a confidence she hadn't felt since first walking through the front door of Whitney Hall.

"What!" Cleve straightened and stared down at her smiling face.

She rose on tiptoe and kissed his cheek. For the second time that night her perfume lingered in his nostrils, filling him with her feminine warmth and loveliness. "Perhaps a few more roses will help me change my mind," she whispered softly.

"You're a tease, Rina Matthews," Cleve called out as she turned and walked towards her bedroom. He registered the seductive sway of her hips under the calf-length gown.

"I thought I was a ninny, Cleveland Whitney," she said over her shoulder.

"You're a ninny and a tease."

"Good night again, Cleve." Turning back, she blew him a kiss..

"Good night, sweet..." His words trailed off as he watched her step inside her bedroom and close the French doors.

He stood in the moonlight for a long time, long after Rina returned to her bed and fell asleep.

CHAPTER 10

Rina felt the power of the Corvette's engine as she shifted gears. Driving this car always gave her a feeling of control; she could go as fast or as slow as she desired. Like her life, she was the only one who could control it, not her family, not Jason.

Savannah was fully awake by the time she maneuvered into a parking lot behind a row of trendy shops in the downtown area.

Half an hour later, after making the transfers at a bank branch, she completed all of her banking transactions. Feeling secure that her business rating would continue unblemished, she strolled leisurely along a street lined with fashionable window displays and colorful awnings. She skirted a stream of water coming from a hose held by a young blond woman.

"Rina!"

The woman calling her name prompted Rina to stop. Her espadrilles were soaked when the hose was directed on to the sidewalk where she stood.

"Babs!"

Barbara Brandt dropped the hose, the force of the water spraying the sidewalk and everything in the path of the writhing length of green rubber tubing.

"Turn it off, Babs," Rina cried out, laughing and shielding her face, while sidestepping the runaway hose.

Barbara turned a knob hidden behind a large planter, stemming the flow of water. Within seconds the two women were in each other's arms, hugging and talking excitedly.

"What are you doing here?" they asked in unison.

She pulled back, smiling. "I asked first."

Barbara looped her arm through Rina's, directing her into a small elegant dress shop. "I live and work here." Her green eyes crinkled in laughter. "Now, what are you doing in Savannah?" She handed her a fluffy terrycloth towel.

Rina blotted droplets of water from her face and hair. "I'm working near Sapelo."

"Sit down," Barbara urged, steering her towards a delicate chair with a yellow and white-striped cushion. She took a matching chair, watching Rina remove her espadrilles and dry her feet.

Rina handed Barbara the towel, smiling warmly. Barbara Brandt hadn't changed since she last saw her. Her face was a bit rounder, as were her hips, but everything that had made the petite natural blond popular in high school was still evident. Her green eyes sparkled like seductive emeralds and her lips were red as cherries.

"How long has it been, Rina? Ten years?"

"Eleven."

Barbara grimaced. "Has it been that long since we graduated high school?" Rina nodded. "Gosh, honey, what have you been up to? Married? Children?"

"I'm not married," she began.

"What happened to Teddy Marshall?"

She pulled her wet blouse away from her midriff. "We lost contact after he went to college. How about you, Babs? You and Peter still together?"

"We're still together. We've been married so long that everyone says we look alike. We have two kids, boys."

"I guess being married more than ten years nowadays is a long time." Rina glanced around the shop. "How long have you worked here?"

Barbara ran her fingers through her short blond hair. "Not long. My mother owns this place, and I help out on the weekends. I get a break from the boys, and she gets to spend time with them."

Barbara stared at Rina, noting she had changed. She did not look any older than she had when they were in high school together; the change had taken place inwardly.

"Tell me about yourself, Rina? What are you doing? How're Miss Gardner and your daddy?"

Rina turned her attention back to Barbara. "My folks are well."

"Did you ever get used to having one of your teachers as a stepmother?"

She smiled. "Yes. Evelyn's great. It's hard for me to think of her as a stepmother when there's only a ten-year difference in our ages."

Evelyn Gardner had been Rina's sixth grade science teacher, and when Gabriel came to school for parents' night he was immediately taken with the young woman who taught his daughter. Evelyn married Gabriel at twenty-one and gave him a son before she turned twenty-two.

"I'm in partnership with someone," Rina continued. "We have a business management firm."

Barbara's pale brows shifted. "A man?"

"Yes, a man."

"Married or single?"

"He's single."

Barbara stood up, "Keep talking, Rina. I'm going to put on some water for tea." She disappeared through a pair of cafe doors at the back of the shop.

"Are you engaged?" Barbara shouted.

"Not yet." Rina stood up and walked over to a rack of formal gowns.

"What are you waiting for?"

She slid gowns flowing from padded hangers across a bar, unable to answer the question.

Barbara stuck her head through the doors, pointing at a rack at the back of the shop. "You're looking in the wrong section. Your size is over here."

Rina moved over and searched the rack. Seeing the froth of silks and satins reminded her that she needed a dress for the ball.

"Do you have anything in either black or white in my size?" she asked Barbara.

Barbara pushed open the doors slowly, her eyes widening in surprise. "Are you looking for a dress for the black and white ball?"

"Yes." She held up a strapless lace gown with black sequin appliqué. "I want a one-of-a-kind creation."

Barbara walked over to Rina, tapping her lightly on the arm. "Tell me, honey, how did you manage to get invited?"

"I'm working for Abigail Whitney." She moved to a full-length mirror, examining the cut of the dress against her body, pushing out her lower lip and shaking her head. "Too provocative."

Barbara crossed her arms under her breasts. "Peter and I are also going."

Now it was Rina's turn to be surprised. "You're involved with the Whitneys?"

"Peter is program director for their radio station."

"Which one?"

"WJAZ-FM."

Rina laughed, her voice light and tinkling. "Talk about coincidence."

Barbara took the dress from her. "Call it fate. We were destined to meet again." She put the dress on the rack. "I may have a delicious little thing that might fit you." She squinted at Rina. "You look like a six," she concluded, disappearing through the cafe doors for a second time.

"I don't want something that a half dozen other women will be wearing," she informed Barbara.

"A half dozen women don't have your waist size, Rina. I think this dress is a four, but there's enough seam to let it out to where it should fit you perfectly."

"There's no way I can fit into…" Her mouth gaped when she saw the dress Barbara cradled across her arm. It was a frothy creation of strapless black silk chiffon with white seed pearls dotting the flowing skirt, bodice and off-the-shoulder pouf sleeves. The bodice was cut on a bias, giving it a swirling effect and dipping lower at the hipline.

"You like it?" Barbara queried, knowing the answer before even asking.

"Where's your fitting room?"

Barbara smiled. "Behind you."

Rina took the dress and walked into the small space lined with wall-to-wall mirrors. She prayed it would fit as she slipped out of her slacks, damp shirt and bra. Yards and yards of black chiffon floated out around her after she had slipped the dress over her head and shoulders.

"Do you need help?" Barbara called out.

She stared at her reflection in the mirror. She had zipped the dress without pulling in her middle. It was a perfect fit. "Come in and look, Babs."

Barbara stepped into the fitting room and met Rina's gaze in the mirror. "Oh my, oh my," she repeated over and over. "It's perfect, honey. It's beautiful. You're beautiful."

Rina fluffed the pouf sleeves, shifting and examining the back of the dress. "I'll take it."

Barbara swallowed hard, grimacing. "It's not cheap, Rina. The pearls are all hand-sewn."

Rina shot Barbara a look of annoyance. "I said I'll take it," she repeated. Lowering her chin, she gave Barbara a narrowed stare. "Have you sold another one like this?"

"Oh no! My mother made this dress for a woman who went to Italy on vacation and never came back. She met an Italian vintner and married him. We just got a card from her last week. She's with child, so this dress is a definite no-no for her."

Rina ran her hands down the bodice. "Let's see what it can do for me."

"Who's the lucky guy?"

"Jason Harper," Rina replied out of habit. She stepped out of the dress, handing it to Barbara.

"Did he go to school with us?"

Rina reached for her blouse. "No. I met him in grad school. He's my business partner."

"That's what I call a smooth transition, from the board room to the bedroom."

Right now Harper and Matthews' boardroom activities were anything but smooth. Jason was not making it easy for her.

She put back on her clothes while Barbara put the dress away. They spent the next hour reminiscing over several cups of herbal tea and scones.

"Even though I'll see you at the black and white ball you still have to come up again and visit," Barbara reminded Rina.

"I have the weekends off, so I'll give you a call and let you know when to expect me," she promised, hugging her former schoolmate. "I'll see you soon. Give my regards to your mother."

"Same to your folks. Don't worry about the dress. I'll have it delivered to Whitney Hall in time for the ball."

Rina left the boutique and spent the rest of the morning browsing in the shopping district. She toured the Oglethorpe Mall, stopping twice at specialty shops to purchase gifts for Evelyn and Emily-Jane.

It was noon by the time she returned to her car to begin the drive that would take her down the coast to Whitney Hall.

CHAPTER 11

Rina returned to Whitney Hall, encountering a flurry of frenzied activity. Cars crowded the driveway and every other patch of paved surface surrounding the large house. People had begun arriving for Cleve's announcement that he was officially declaring his candidacy for mayor of Savannah.

She walked into the house, pushing her way through the crowd milling about the living room. Rina caught a quick glimpse of the live-in housekeeper's pink uniform before she disappeared behind the sliding doors to the dining room.

Rina made her way up the stairs and down the hall to her bedroom. "Where have you been?"

Rina stopped short, staring up at a frowning Cleve as he walked out of the bedroom next to hers. A delicate eyebrow arched. "Excuse me, Mr. Whitney," she drawled in a sarcastic tone.

Cleve ran a hand over his face and let out his breath. His hand fell away and she recognized the ravages of strain for the first time. Lines of fatigue ringed his generous mouth and a slight puffiness narrowed his usually intense eyes.

"I thought you were going to miss my official announcement," he explained.

Nonplussed, she said, "You don't need me for that."

Cleve's dark gaze swept over the hair pulled back off her forehead in a single braid falling down her back and the satiny sheen of her unmade face. The frantic searching of his eyes stilled, moving with agonizing slowness over her features, as if committing each one to memory.

"Yes," he said after what seemed an interminable silence. "Yes, I do, Rina."

Something in his tone, his stance, went out to her; and what she did not know was that for the first time in Cleveland Whitney's life he was reaching out for something, for someone. Under his facade of complete control and ongoing successes was a man who was afraid for the first time in his life, afraid of obtaining and losing the only thing he wanted more than his own life.

Rina took in his casual khaki slacks, light blue short sleeve shirt and imported dark brown loafers.

"When are you scheduled to make the announcement?

"In forty minutes," he replied, not looking at his watch.

The cacophony of human voices escalated from the first floor, but the large house could have been empty and silent as Rina and Cleve stared at each other, intuitively acknowledging the other's thoughts, the other's raw, hidden emotions.

Her lids lowered as a knowing smile softened her mouth. "I'll be ready."

Cleve's left hand went to her neck, his fingers grazing the soft curly hair on her nape. She shivered as he tightened his grip. Lowering his head, he moved closer. "Thank you, Rina," he whispered, his clean breath warm and moist against her lips.

Rina went still. The urge to raise her face, her lips, to his was strong and reckless. She wanted his kiss, his fiery touch. "I must change," she said instead. "Please let me go, Cleve."

He loosened his grip, but didn't release her. "One of these days you're going to beg me to hold you, Rina."

The magic vanished; the moment was gone. The man's arrogance irked her. "Don't count on it, Cleve."

His hand fell away as he moved back. "I'm more certain of that than any other thing in my life. So certain," he continued quietly, "that I would risk everything I possess on it."

"Then you're about to lose, Cleveland Whitney," she shot back with a half-smile.

He gave her a maddening grin. "You would be worth it, Rina Matthews. Every dollar and every penny."

"Even the election?" she asked. When he didn't reply she turned and made her way to her bedroom, opening the door and closing it softly, not hearing him whisper, "Even the election."

She placed the decorative shopping bag with Emily-Jane's coloring book, crayons and a small, stuffed teddy bear on the rocker and kicked off her shoes.

Sitting on the side of her bed, she stripped off her clothes. The soft smile playing at the corners of her mouth became a wide grin when she spied the crystal vase filled with a bouquet of white roses nestled with delicate baby's breath; and she knew that Cleve giving her roses was no longer a peace offering but something more.

One of these days you're going to beg me to hold you, Rina. His words were branded on her brain and in her heart.

Everything that was Cleveland Whitney was seeping into her being, filling her with his dynamic presence, his sensual existence. What she felt for him was puzzling and foreign.

When had she become so conscious of the deep passions within her? Why was it becoming more difficult to deny the sexual cravings that surfaced when she least expected them? How long could she lie to herself and say she loved Jason Harper? How long could she continue to deny herself the act that had become as necessary as eating and sleeping?

She rose and made her way to the bathroom. One thing she was certain of was that when she spoke to Jason again it would serve a two-fold purpose. And both would concern their future.

Rina checked her hair in a mirror, tucking an errant curl into the twist of hair on the nape other neck.

Turning slightly, she noted her reflection. She had selected an off-white silk slip dress with a pleated skirt, pairing it with a matching off-white cotton and silk blend crocheted pullover. Her sun-browned skin showed through the delicate lace like swirls of burnished satin.

Slipping her bare feet into a pair of white leather flats, she rechecked the clock on the mantel. Cleve was scheduled to announce his candidacy in five minutes.

Her gaze lingered longingly on the profusion of flowers as she backed out of the room, plowing into him.

She gasped loudly as his hands went to her waist, but she did not protest nor pull away. Cleve turned her gently in the circle of his strong arms.

"I didn't mean to startle you, but I have to talk to you before we go downstairs," he apologized, leading her slowly down the hall.

Rina sensed his disquiet. "What about?"

A tall young man raced down the hall towards them, preempting Cleve's reply. "Come on, brother, the press is waiting for you." He whistled softly under his breath when he spied Rina. "Definitely worth the wait," he mumbled, nodding in approval.

Cleve's fingers tightened on Rina's waist. "Rina, this is my brother, Rubel. Rube, Rina Matthews."

She smiled at Rubel, and she was rewarded with a boyish, lopsided grin.

Rubel fell in step with Rina and his older brother, and she was acutely aware of the marked resemblance between the two men: tall, broad-shouldered, a rich dark coloring and intense dark eyes.

Rubel studied Rina's profile. "Mother can't stop talking about you," he remarked. "She claims you're going to work miracles with her finances."

"I'm afraid your mother's a bit premature," she replied modestly. "I intend to conduct an audit of the past two years, then submit a report with my recommendations. That will be the extent of my miracle work."

"After you finish with Mother, perhaps you'll consider handling some of my personal holdings," Rubel continued as if she hadn't spoken.

"You'll have to wait, Rube," Cleve said with cool authority. He stopped at the top of the curving staircase, staring down at the people waiting patiently for him. His gaze swung back to his brother, then Rina. "I want to ask Rina if she would manage my campaign finances." Rubel nodded and made his way down the stairs, acknowledging his older brother's dismissal.

The shock of Cleve's request chilled the words locked in Rina's throat. Cleve held her arm and led her more than halfway down the stairs before she finally found her voice.

"Cleve…I can't."

"Why not?" he whispered loudly. "Your firm doesn't need the money or the additional publicity?"

Of course her firm could use the money, but it would also mean that her association with Cleve

Whitney would not end in two months, but in November.

"I'll discuss it with you later," she replied as scores of reporters and photographers gathered at the foot of the staircase.

His hold on her arm tightened. "It has to be now, Rina. The press wouldn't want to come back here for a repeat performance."

Her nerves tensed immediately. "Why didn't you ask me earlier?"

Cleve motioned to a reporter from a large Savannah daily. "Give me another minute." He turned his attention back to Rina. "I'd hoped it wouldn't come to this, but I just got a call from the firm who consented to handle my campaign finances. They've decided to go with Ross."

The strain Rina had noticed earlier was now more apparent. A muscle twitched noticeably in his jaw as his breathing became more labored. Cleveland Whitney, who never needed anyone, needed her; and Harper and Matthews needed the revenue. Not once did she think she needed Cleveland Whitney.

"Rina," he moaned, as if in agony.

"I'll do it," she said, committing herself to his political future.

"Thank you, sweetheart. Thank you so very, very much."

She patted his shoulder. "You're welcome. Now, go tell these people what they've come to hear."

Cleve led Rina to a small group gathered in a corner of the living room, then moved over to a pair of loveseats set up in the middle of the expansive room.

She watched Cleve, ignoring the hushed whispers going on around her from the members of his campaign committee. He appeared controlled and relaxed as he answered the questions put to him from a popular television news correspondent. He draped one leg over the other, smiling and gesturing naturally.

Her gaze moved slowly around the room, noting the petite photographer who had taken her photograph at The Crab Shack. She flashed Rina a smile, nodding. Rina returned the nod. So far the picture she had taken of them had not appeared in the papers.

Rina also recognized the young woman she had seen the first day she arrived at Whitney Hall. Maddie Jackson sat on a chair, holding Emily-Jane on her lap. Emily-Jane's chubby legs and sandaled feet crossed and uncrossed in nervous energy.

Abigail gave up her chair to a very pregnant young woman who eased her swollen bulk down slowly to the brocade cushioned seat.

Cleve's interview continued as reporters positioned their hand-held tape recorders, while camera people positioned video cameras on their shoulders or tripods. In ten minutes it was over.

Rina and the other members of the election team were huddled together for a group picture. It was a relaxed, informal session, with everyone laughing and hugging. Photographers identified each one for their picture captions, while Cleve exchanged parting remarks with his interviewer before making his way across the room to his specially selected team. He appeared more relaxed than he had before Rina had accepted becoming his finance manager.

His gaze caught hers over the heads of several shorter men and held. His compelling eyes were filled with a deep longing, and Rina felt his quiet assurance, his self-confidence.

Cleve slipped his hands into the pockets of his slacks, smiling at her. There was a lazy seductiveness in the smile and much more; and she thought she caught a look of supreme victory before he turned to answer a question put to him by the photographer who had caught them in the intimate pose only two days ago.

"Rina?"

She turned at the sound of Abigail's voice and smiled at Cleve's mother. "It's official now, Abigail."

Abigail looped her arm through Rina's, steering her away from the crush of campaign workers and members of the press. "I do want to personally thank you for helping Cleveland. I've never seen my son carry on the way he did when he got the call from that firm who promised to handle his campaign finances. Cleveland had heard the rumors that they were going to defect, but he refused to believe them until this morning."

"I guess it's become a case of poetic justice," Rina replied, leaning closer to Abigail. "Cleve opposed my coming here to work for you, and now he has to humble himself and ask my help."

Abigail gave Rina a sidelong glance. "Cleveland was humbled the first time he saw you, Rina. You're the first woman who has attempted to meet him as an equal."

"I don't enjoy sparring with him," she admitted honestly.

"No more than he enjoys baiting you, child. I want so much for you to be friends. You seem so suited for each other. You're a much better choice than Paige would've ever been for my son," Abigail added. "Come, let me introduce you to my family."

Rina wondered who Paige was. She did not have time to dwell on Abigail's statement, however, as she was suddenly surrounded by Whitneys of every age, height and differing looks. Emily-Jane grasped her hand and pulled her over to her mother.

"Mama, this is my friend, Rina."

Maddie pressed her cheek to Rina's in an affectionate gesture. "Welcome to the family." She laid a manicured hand on the arm of a tall, slender man who appeared at least twice her age. "This is my husband, Darren Jackson, Darling, Rina Matthews."

Darren's smoldering dark eyes lingered a moment on Rina's face, then shifted somewhere over her head. "Nice meeting you, Rina," he drawled as if bored by all of the excitement going on around him.

Rina nodded. "Darren." She noted that his relaxed, subdued personality seemed totally incongruent with Maddie's bubbling effervescence.

She discovered the pregnant woman was Philip Whitney's wife, Carole. Philip stood behind Carole's chair, both hands resting lightly on her shoulders.

"Jason Harper may say a lot of things, but he did not lie about you, Rina," Philip remarked with a wide rakish grin. "He's a lucky man."

A dizzying current raced through Rina, but she did not have to turn around to know Cleve was behind her. Without looking, she felt his presence, his energy, and she silently thanked Cleve for his sudden appearance. She did not want to discuss Jason with Philip.

"Have you met everyone?" Cleve asked close to her ear.

Shifting slightly, she smiled up at him. "I met your sister, brothers, Darren and Carole."

Cleve moved over and kissed Carole's cheek. "You look wonderful."

Carole frowned. "I look fat?"

Cleve patted her cheek. "You're beautifully pregnant, Carole."

"It'll be over soon, cupcake," Philip reassured his wife. He hunkered down beside her chair, consoling her.

Cleve straightened, his right arm curving around Rina's waist and molding her soft curves to his side. "Come with me," he whispered. "I want to talk to you, alone."

Rina followed him through the crowd still lingering in the living room, noting their curious stares. He led her into her office, and she watched as he closed the door behind them. Leaning against the door, hands in his pockets, Cleve smiled.

She stood facing him, returning his smile. "What do you want to talk about?"

His smile slipped away. The shaft of sunlight streaming into the room bathed Rina in gold. It reflected off the tawny golden skin shimmering through the lacy pullover. It glinted off the streaks in her hair, and it caught the brilliant lights in her luminous eyes.

Cleve pushed away from the door, moving as silently as a large cat. "I must thank you for what you've done for me."

She was rooted to the spot, unable to move. His steady gaze bore into her with silent expectation, and she knew what was going to happen before he reached for her.

Rina moved into his embrace. Gently, deliberately, Cleve pulled her closer until their hearts melded in a strong, steady, measured beating.

Rina's lids fluttered over her eyes. "Cleveland," she moaned.

His mouth covered hers hungrily, exploring and drawing from her what she would have freely given if only he had asked. Her lips parted under his as the heat from his mouth flared into hers, filling her entire being with Cleveland Whitney's raw maleness.

His embrace, his kiss was so different, so foreign that Rina felt herself drowning in the feel and smell of the man holding her to his heart.

His tongue slipped between her teeth, searching, moving in and out of her hot, moist mouth, the motion precipitating a sensual throbbing in another part of her body, a secret, hidden place.

His lips moved from her mouth to her throat, leaving streaks of fire across her mouth.

"Thank you, sweetheart," he murmured hoarsely, placing tender kisses down the column of her slender neck. "Thank you, thank you, thank you," he whispered over and over, kissing her ear, her nape and her shoulders.

Rina felt the heat through the lace of her pullover. Cleve's head dipped lower, his mouth settling over a breast. She felt her knees weaken when the nipple hardened against the silk of the slip.

One of his hands covered the other breast, the gentle massage of his fingers sending red-hot currents of desire through her.

His kiss, his touch made her feel like a slow moving drop of heated wax making its way down the slender length of a flaming candle. She melted into him, breathing lightly between parted lips.

Cleve's hands moved over all of her pleasure points, short-circuiting her control. His fingers caught the skirt of her dress, gathering fabric while he bared her thighs. "Oh…" Her cry was cut off as he again took possession of her mouth.

His fingers caressed the smooth, silken flesh of her inner thigh, moving inexorably upward. His hand seared a fiery path over satin bikinis and her flat abdomen.

Instinctively, her body arched toward him, wanting to get closer. She desperately wanted to get closer; she needed him; she wanted him.

Rina was sailing, floating high above reality. Nothing mattered; nothing mattered except that she felt free, freer than at any other time in her life.

She was fully aware of his hardness pressing against her thighs, and somehow reality returned with a jolting clarity. She struggled to free her mind and body from Cleve's sensual grip. It had gone too far.

She extracted her mouth, pushing against his hard chest. "No. No more."

The heat lingered in her face as she felt his gaze on her lowered head. Cleve had aroused her to peaks of desire she hadn't thought possible.

"Go," she whispered, her voice trembling uncontrollably. "Please!"

Cleve stared at Rina for a long time, then released her, turning and walking out of the room, closing the door softly behind him.

Rina made it to an armchair on shaking knees and sat, burying her face in her hands.

How had she let it get so out of hand? Why hadn't she stopped him?

But hadn't she been the slightest bit curious? Curious enough to know how it would be to make love to Cleveland Whitney?

Hadn't she unconsciously fantasized about a mysterious stranger making love to her in a garden or meadow of white flowers?

And didn't she want that stranger to be Cleve?

Yes! Yes! Yes! Her mind screamed. She wanted Cleve to make love to her; she wanted the stranger in her dream to be him; and she knew beyond all hope that she was inexorably caught in the spell he had woven.

The telephone rang, reminding her of where and who she was. She was in her office at Whitney Hall; she was an accountant; she had been hired to audit Mrs. Abigail Whitney's holdings.

The ringing continued and Rina moved from the chair to answer the telephone.

"Rina Matthews." She did not recognize her own voice. It sounded too low, too detached.

"Rina, it's Jason."

Her pulse began racing again, but for a different reason. With Cleve it has been in passion; with Jason it was anger.

"Bill Newton called me," she began. "And…"

"I've taken care of that, Rina," Jason came back in a cold tone, interrupting her. "I deposited a check from Tom Garritson this morning."

"He gave you his account?" Her voice rose in surprise.

"Did you think he wouldn't?" Jason questioned. There was a hint of arrogance in his tone. "Look, Rina, I thought we agreed that I would handle the marketing and PR."

She felt her own temper flare. "Handling marketing and PR does not extend to overdrawing our account, Jason. Why didn't you let me know that you intended to lease a new car?"

Jason let out an audible sigh. "I didn't think it was necessary, Rina."

"Why not, Jason? We're supposed to be partners."

"We are partners. But you have to let me do my thing. You can't stifle me or I can't do what do best, Rina. And that means bringing in the money to cover all expenses."

She felt what was close to hysteria. "I transferred monies from my personal account this morning to cover expenses for our business."

"You didn't have to do that!" he shouted. "The retainer from Garritson was more than enough to cover all business expenses for the next two months."

"I did not know that, Jason. Perhaps if you would call me on a regular basis I'd know what the hell is going on back in Atlanta."

There was a noticeable pause. "Look, baby, let's not fight with each other. I know working under Cleveland's intimidation hasn't been easy, but stay calm, baby. In less than two months you'll out of there and the man will be a bad memory."

Rina's body prickled with heat in remembrance of Cleve's lovemaking. "It's not Cleveland Whitney, Jason."

"Good," Jason replied quickly. "Look, baby, I have to hang up. The Garritsons are giving a little something this afternoon and I have to get ready. I'll call you Monday morning."

"Jason…"

"Hush now, baby. All I want you to know is that I love you, and I can't wait until we're married."

The line went dead, leaving Rina listening to the dial tone. She hung up, struggling not to react to Jason's declaration of love as mixed feelings surged through her.

Closing her eyes, she bit down hard on her lower lip. *Don't love me, Jason,* she thought. She didn't want him to love her. Jason did not excite her; he did not make her feel special; but more than that, he did not make her feel like a woman.

Reopening her eyes, she stared out at the striped wallpaper. Cleve made her feel everything she should have felt with Jason.

She thought of her response to Cleve's lovemaking and her body reacted violently as she relived the feel of his sensual mouth, the sweeping, searching exploration of his hands and the unyielding hardness of his male body.

Sighing heavily, she stood up. She couldn't hide out in her office for the rest of the afternoon. She had to face Cleve; and she would also let him know what had occurred between them would not and could not happen again.

CHAPTER 12

Rina walked into the living room and found it empty except for the housekeeper. Mrs. Wells was straightening a side table at its proper angle.

"Did everyone leave?" Rina asked.

Mrs. Wells glanced up, smiling. "Sakes no, child. They're all outside. There's going to be a lot of celebratin' before this day's over."

She thanked Mrs. Wells, making her way outdoors. As a member of the campaign team she knew she was expected to put in an occasional appearance at the political gatherings.

Bright sunlight and warm breezes set the stage for the near one hundred people sitting on chairs, benches and on the lawns surrounding the two-hundred-year-old structure. Caterers had set up large yellow-and-white-striped tents from which different aromas wafted in the summer air.

"Oh, there you are, Rina. I was just coming to get you."

Rina noted the slight frown marring Abigail's smooth forehead. "Is something wrong, Abigail?"

The frown disappeared. "No. I asked Cleveland where you were and he said you were in your office. It was my understanding you would not work on the weekend."

"I had to talk to Jason," she said quickly.

Abigail peered closely at the younger woman's strained expression. "Is everything all right between you and your partner?" she asked perceptively.

"Yes." And it was, for now.

"There are other Whitneys I want you to meet," Abigail said, taking her arm. "It seems all of the family has turned out to help Cleveland kick off his campaign."

She was introduced to cousins three and four generations removed. Anyone with a drop of Whitney blood had come to Whitney Hall for the celebration, and she noted that some of the press corps had also elected to stay.

A disc jockey arrived and set up a sound system, playing various forms of pop music. The sounds of laughter, crying babies and giggling adolescents mingled with the music, all adding to the festive occasion.

Rina caught a glimpse of Cleve as he stopped and exchanged pleasantries with his guests. His gaze caught hers, lingered, then dropped when his attention was diverted elsewhere.

She made her way to the striped tent and filled a plate with a sampling of barbecue chicken, spareribs and crab, okra gumbo. She also spooned a serving of green tomato relish and chow-chow onto her plate.

The caterers also offered a selection of broiled lobster tails, shrimp and soft shell crabs in addition to the quintessential hamburgers and grilled frank-furters. The cold dishes included deviled eggs with anchovies, apple-walnut salad, cabbage and chicken salads, and Southern-style potato salad.

She balanced her plate and glass of iced tea while making her way to a stone bench under the sweeping branches of an ancient live oak tree. A shadow fell over her. She looked up, her heart lurching and thudding wildly in her chest.

"May I join you?" Cleve asked, balancing his own plate. He did not wait for her response, sitting down close, too close, to her.

She stared at his strong profile. "Yes, Cleveland Whitney, you may sit with me."

Cleve winked at her. "Thanks, sweetheart."

She went rigid. "Please don't call me that."

He broke off a piece of cornbread, chewing it slowly, his eyes never leaving her face. "Why not?" he asked after swallowing. "Does Harper call you that?"

"Jason has nothing to do with you calling me sweetheart."

Cleve leaned closer and pressed a kiss to her temple. Her body's heat and the sensual scent of her perfume lingered in his nostrils.

"I like calling you sweetheart," he murmured. Rina stared at him. His expression revealed he wasn't teasing.

"I want to hold you again, Rina," he confessed in a low, thick tone repressed with sexual tension. "I want to touch you and kiss you and make certain I haven't dreamt you."

No, her heart screamed. She closed her eyes, a hand tightening on her fork. "Don't do this to me, Cleve."

He registered her look of agony. "Don't do what, darling?"

Rina leaned toward him, resting her head on his shoulder. "Don't make me choose, because I can't."

Cleve put down his plate and cradled Rina gently within his strong arms. "I'll wait, Rina," he whispered in her hair. "I'll wait for you."

Instead of joy, she felt pain. "Don't…"

"Sweetheart," he crooned, not allowing her to finish her statement. "Harper is going to slip up, big time. And when he does I'll be there for you. Even if you marry him I'll wait. I…"

Rina raised her head, pressing her fingertips to his lips, stopping his words. "No, Cleve! You're not being fair to me. You expect me to go into a marriage knowing you want me. And every time I take off my clothes and lie with Jason will I fantasize that it's you that I'm making love to and not my husband? And if I become pregnant, do I pray that it's your child I'm carrying beneath my heart and not his?"

Cleve's expression hardened as he stared down at her. He grasped her hand firmly. "I am being fair to you."

"You aren't," she countered. "You're using me to get back at Jason because you don't like him."

"I am not using you, Rina." There was a cold edge to his words.

"Are you or are you not trying to seduce me to get back at Jason?"

"No," he mumbled savagely.

Her eyebrows lifted. "No, what, Cleve?" Cleve released her hand, turning away. He refused to answer, incensing her.

"Don't bother to wait for me, Cleveland Whitney, because two lifetimes wouldn't be long enough."

His temper exploded as he turned back to face her. "You're talking out of both sides of your mouth, Rina. You want me! You want me as much as I want you, but you're too much of a coward to admit it. Your passion gives you away, sweetheart. I've tasted your mouth and your body and you give as well as you take."

"I don't want you," she lied smoothly.

Cleve stared at her, then burst out laughing.

"You beautiful, sexy little liar. Do you want me to show you how much you don't want me?"

Rina matched his smile with a cynical one of her own. "Drop dead," she crooned.

"Only after I've made love to you," he retorted with a sinister grin. "But I prefer another kind of death, Rina Matthews. I'm sure you're more than familiar with *le petit mort.*"

It was Rina's turn not to respond. How could she respond to what was called the little death when she had not yet experienced sexual fulfillment?

Instead, she concentrated on eating the food on her plate, not looking at Cleve again. He picked up his own fork and they finished eating in complete silence.

He watched her wipe her mouth with a napkin, visibly admiring the delicate bones that made up her face, the slender curve of her long neck and the tanned honey-gold hues in her brown skin.

Taking her plate, he stacked it on his. "Are you ready to walk off your food?"

His gaze was soft and gentle as a caress, and she stared back at him with longing. Her lips were silent, while her heart pumped yes, yes, yes with every life-sustaining beat.

"Your guests will miss you," she said softly.

"My guests are family. They'll forgive me," he replied, smiling.

Cleve took her hand as they made their way through the boxwood gardens and orchards. Fruit trees were putting forth their summer yield of apples, peaches, pears and cherries.

"This land is a botanist's dream," she remarked when she stopped and stared back at the portion of grounds the Whitneys had permitted to remain in its natural state.

He nodded in agreement. "It's wild, but there's something reverent about seeing the land as God intended it to be."

Rina ran her fingertips over a profusion of white foxglove spires growing from a thick hedge.

His larger hand covered hers. Turning her into the circle of his embrace, Cleve held her gently, his lips pressing lightly to her forehead.

He felt the rapid beating of her heart against his own. "You could stay here forever, Rina," he whispered, repeating the words she had spoken the night before. "All you have to do is say it, sweetheart, and I'll grant your wish."

Rina refused to listen to her heart; she refused to believe that she was falling in love with Cleveland Whitney.

"Let's go back," she insisted.

He pulled back and stared down at the shimmering pools of green and gold staring up at him. "Will you attend church services with the family tomorrow morning?"

Her eyes crinkled with her smile. "Yes."

He pulled her hand into the curve of his elbow, leading her back across the meadow of wildflowers. "Mother insists we share breakfast together on Sunday mornings before we all go to church. We eat at eight and leave around ten-thirty for the eleven o'clock service," Cleve informed Rina as they approached Whitney Hall.

Both of them discovered their absence had not been that apparent. Rina spent the rest of the afternoon and early evening socializing with the visiting Whitneys. Most were friendly, outgoing and unpretentious. A few of the male adolescents flirted shamelessly with her as Cleve observed the interchange. It seemed as if each time she turned, Cleve was less than ten feet away. He was not going to let her out of his line of vision.

The caterers cleared away trays of food, then collapsed the large tents. Long after they had cleaned up and left, the humid night air held the lingering aroma of cooked food.

The sky turned a fiery shade of crimson and orange as the sun sank down behind a copse of trees. Babies slept soundly on their mothers' laps, while elderly relatives retreated to the house, away from the noise and music blaring from the speakers set up outdoors. Lovers of all ages slipped surreptitiously off into the quiet seclusion of the woods and gardens for an interlude of stolen rapture.

Rina wanted to be one of those lovers; she wanted to steal away with Cleve and offer him what she had never offered any other man: all of herself. Not only her body, but also her heart.

Night had descended by the time she climbed the curving staircase and walked the hail to her bedroom. She lay on her bed in the darkened room, staring at the ceiling.

She was falling in love with a stranger; a man she had known less than a week. Cleveland Whitney had taken her heart and refused to return it to her.

And how she wished she knew if what he felt for her was more than lust. What was it about her, other than her face, that attracted him?

Rina sat up suddenly, breathing heavily. Everything that had occurred since she arrived at Whitney Hall flashed back like images on a screen.

Cleve had given in too easily. He was used to winning, not losing, and when he conceded after she threatened him with a lawsuit for defaming her character she had willingly accepted it.

She recalled his comment regarding Jason. *I don't like threats, Rina.*

Jason was Cleve's target, not hers. If Cleve could seduce her away from Jason, then he would have gained another victory. He wanted to humiliate Jason; he wanted to bring Jason to his knees with a personal victory when he took the woman he coveted away from him. If successful, then Cleveland Whitney would continue his string of winning every case he brought to trial, in or out of the courtroom.

Not with my help, Rina thought. If Cleve wanted to destroy Jason he would do it without her assistance.

CHAPTER 13

"Hi, Rina," Emily-Jane squealed excitedly as Rina entered the breakfast room. The child slipped off her chair and ran over to Rina, arms extended.

Rina went to her knees, pulling Emily-Jane to her chest. She kissed the little girl's silky brown cheek. "How are you this morning?"

Emily-Jane's chubby arms tightened around her neck. "I'm okay. Uncle Cleve reads the stories good now," she whispered in Rina's ear.

"Good for him," she whispered back.

A pair of long male legs came into Rina's line of vision. She recognized the muscled calves and strong ankles immediately.

"Good morning, Cleve," she said from her kneeling position.

Cleve towered above Rina and Emily-Jane, hands on his hips, smiling. Emily-Jane released Rina's neck, and he extended a hand, helping her to rise smoothly.

"Good morning, sweetheart."

Emily-Jane blinked up at her uncle. "Her name is not sweetheart, Uncle Cleve. Her name is Rina."

Cleve released Rina's hand. Bending slightly, he swung his niece up into his arms. Pressing his forehead to hers, he kissed her nose. "I call Rina sweetheart because I like her very much."

Emily-Jane's arms curved around his strong neck. "You like her like you like me?"

Cleve stared at Rina, holding her captive with his intense, dark eyes. "I like Rina the way I like you, Em-Jay, but differently."

Emily-Jane looked from Rina to Cleve. "How different, Uncle Cleve?"

His gaze swung back to his niece's animated features. "You probably won't understand the difference until you're older."

"And you'd better be a lot older, Emily-Jane Whitney Jackson," Maddie stated, walking into the breakfast room. She had overheard the conversation between her brother and daughter. She held out her arms for Emily-Jane, and Cleve handed the child to her.

Rina hid a smile as she turned to the buffet server to choose her breakfast. Emily-Jane had put Cleve on the spot, where he had to explain the endearment he used as freely as taking his next breath.

She handed him her plate when he moved over to stand beside her. Her smile was sensual and mischievous. "Will you please fix my plate, sweetheart?" She told him she wanted pancakes, a beef sausage and coffee.

"See, Mama," Emily-Jane called out, pointing. "Rina and Uncle Cleve don't know their own names. They call each other sweetheart."

"It's all right, baby," Maddie urged, tying a cloth napkin around her daughter's neck. "Sweetheart is a secret word between your uncle Cleve and Rina," she added.

Rina sat down at the table, winking at Maddie. "Who's a sweetheart?" Rubel questioned, escorting Abigail into the sun-filled room.

Maddie cast Cleve a sidelong glance. "Your eldest brother."

"Whose sweetheart are you, big brother?" Rubel asked, seating Abigail at her place at the head of the table.

"Rina's," Maddie and Emily-Jane chorused in unison.

Rina lowered her gaze, staring at the tablecloth. The heat rose in her face, and she wished she was anywhere but at the Whitney breakfast table.

Cleve seemed unaffected by all of the talk about him, while Abigail appeared quite amused by the interchange.

Philip entered the room, followed by Darren. Like Rina, everyone was casually dressed. T-shirts, shorts, sandals and casual slacks and dresses were in evidence.

The only exception was Darren Jackson. Even though it was early morning, he appeared elegant and fastidious in a pair of white linen slacks and a white shirt in a finely woven gauze cotton. And unlike the other men, he had shaved and groomed his hair to perfection.

"Carole wants breakfast in bed this morning," Philip announced, preparing a tray for his pregnant wife.

Abigail accepted a plate from Rubel, thanking him with a warm smile. "Is Carole feeling poorly, Philip?"

"No, Mother. She just needs a little spoiling, that's all," Philip replied.

"I think cupcake is spoiled enough, Philip," Rubel teased, giving his brother a saccharin grin.

"Wait until you're married, little brother," Philip warned.

"I don't think so," Rubel returned. He pulled one of Emily-Jane's braids as he sat down beside her. Leaning over, he placed a noisy kiss on his niece's cheek. "You look beautiful this morning, Em-Jay."

Emily-Jane blew him a noisy kiss. "You always say that, Uncle Rube."

Rubel wiggled his eyebrows, "Well, you do. The most beautiful women in the world are seated right here at this table. Don't you agree, Cleve?"

Cleve sat down opposite Rina, his gaze trained on her face. His mouth quirked as he noted the color darkening her cheeks. "Amen, brother."

"Well, since everyone's here I want you all to know that Darren and I are expecting another baby," Maddie announced proudly.

There was complete silence as the Whitneys stared at Darren. Philip stopped filling a plate for Carole, a look of surprise freezing his expression.

"Now, how did you manage that, Darren?" Cleve questioned.

Philip handed Darren his plate. "Permit me to serve you, my man. I'm certain you need to regain your strength after working that hard to get my sister pregnant again."

Darren stared down at the plate, a half-smile curving his mouth. Shifting his shoulders in a nonchalant gesture, he picked up a cup of steaming, fragrant coffee, unaffected by Cleve's and Philip's teasing.

"He should work that hard at the station," Rubel grumbled. "Our dear brother-in-law hasn't been in his office for weeks. I'm certain he can't even remember the color of his new carpet."

Rina was shocked at the reactions of the Whitney brothers.

She thought they would have extended congratulations instead of barbs. It was apparent they were not too pleased with Maddie's choice in a husband.

"Don't be cruel, Rube," Maddie retorted, scowling. "Lest you forget, it was Darren who was responsible for your attending the Alexander soiree. And it was you and not Darren who wanted to meet Miss Vanessa Alexander," she argued, defending her husband.

"I hired Darren to be a radio programmer, not a social connoisseur," Rube countered angrily.

"You're being unfair to Darren," Maddie shot back.

"Unfair!" Rube sputtered. "If he wasn't your husband and Emily-Jane's father I would've fired him the first day. He showed up a week late at the station," he added under his breath.

"Enough," Abigail announced with quiet authority. "Good wishes are in order." She smiled at Maddie, then Darren. "Thank you for giving me another grandchild."

Darren displayed a slow smile, motioning with his raised cup. "Thank you, Mother, Cleveland, Philip and Rubel."

Philip reached over and reclaimed his plate. "Get up and fix your own, brother."

Cleve stood up and walked over to Darren. He placed a large, well-groomed hand on his brother-in-law's shoulder. "Nice work, Darren."

Darren stared up at Cleve, then rose and extended his right hand. "Thanks, Cleve."

Darren's hand was long and slender, his nails manicured and highly buffed.

Philip and Rubel reluctantly extended their good wishes to Darren. The three Whitney men hugged and kissed Maddie, teasing her until she hid her face in her napkin. Within minutes the tense situation was over.

Breakfast ended an hour later when everyone retreated to their rooms to prepare for church.

Cleve waited for Rina when she walked out of her bedroom, offering his arm. Her fingers curved over the crisp fabric of his white shirt as he fed her down the hall.

"Good morning, love," he crooned, staring down at her expertly applied makeup. Muted colors of pale peach and soft bronze shaded her lids, complimenting the creamy tangerine of her lush, full mouth.

"First sweetheart and now love?" she asked, raising her eyebrows.

"You could be, Rina," Cleve said in a soft voice. "Becoming involved with me may not be too bad a proposition."

"No thanks," she replied. She had no wish to play into Cleve's hands. She would not permit herself to become a pawn in his scheme to topple Jason.

He escorted her down the staircase. "Why do you fight against what is so natural?"

Her fingers gripped his arm, and she hoped he would not notice the spiraling uneasiness she always experienced when he read her so clearly. She did not want to be that transparent.

"Slow down, Cleveland. If you don't stop chasing me, you're not going to have any energy left for your campaign."

"Not only will I have the energy, Rina, but I'll also win both contests," he replied with a deep chuckle. "And what I'm going to enjoy more than taking Ross's seat is proving to you how wrong you are."

She understood his intent immediately. "I'm not a part of the prize package, Cleve."

He stopped at the foot of the staircase, placing both hands on her shoulders. He bent over slightly, and Rina thought he was going to kiss her.

"You're right about that, sweetheart. You are the prize."

It was out in the open. He had said it. He wanted her, and his admission sent her pulse racing.

"Why me, Cleve?"

She felt as if her composure was under attack as he stared at her, unblinking. His hands came down slowly.

"Why not you, Rina? You're exciting, highly intelligent, stimulating, beautiful, elegant…"

"Stop," she interrupted, laughing.

"And sexy," he added with a smile.

She pursed her lips, lowering her chin. "Sexy last?" she teased.

Cleve's smile faded. "No, Rina. You're sexy first. More sexy and passionate than even you know."

Her chin came up and she stared into the black depths of his eyes. Cleveland Whitney radiated a power that drew her to him like a magnet. His arrogance maddened her, but something in his manner soothed and comforted her, something that didn't force her to compete with him, or he with her, something that beckoned to her and let her know that she could be secure and protected with this man.

What she was feeling for Cleve, was that the missing component in her relationship with Jason?

Self-assurance. Self-confidence. It was so natural for Cleve, while Jason struggled continually to obtain it.

Her heart pounded and her head spun wildly. From the very beginning Cleve had lit a fire with in her, stoked it, and now it was blazing out of control; and for the first time Rina did not have a comeback.

And Cleve sensed her acquiescence. "I think we're beginning to understand one another," he stated with a finality neither could dispute.

Cleve led her out of the house and to his car. The jacket to his light gray suit lay across the rear seat. He helped her into the coupe, then slid onto the seat beside her. His gaze swept appreciatively over her face and body, silently admiring her flattering pale orange linen dress.

"You look very nice this morning."

"Thank you," she mumbled, staring out through the windshield.

The back of his right hand moved slowly over her hair. "I like it when you wear your hair down. The different shades are fascinating."

Rina turned and smiled at him, the blown-out waves rippling over her shoulders, as his entranced stare drank in her delicate femininity.

"Thank you."

His gaze dropped to the moist lushness of her mouth. He leaned toward her, then pulled back at the last moment. She didn't realize she had been holding her breath until he secured his seat belt. She exhaled with a soft sigh when he started the engine.

Cleve drove quickly and expertly, leaving Whitney Hall and its environs behind. Rina enjoyed watching the topography change from the thick undergrowth of natural trailing vines and shrubs to ageless trees draped in Spanish moss. The moss always reminded her of a tattered, faded wedding gown.

"You're very quiet, darling," Cleve remarked, taking a quick glance at her averted profile.

"I'm sightseeing. This part of Georgia is so different from Atlanta."

"Do you like it?"

Rina turned back to him, smiling. "Very much."

"Do you still want to stay here? Forever?"

Her smile vanished quickly. "I can't."

He concentrated on his driving, his jaw tightening. "You can't, or you won't?"

"I can't, Cleve," Rina answered firmly.

"So beautiful and so stubborn," he mused aloud. "Just remember one thing, sweetheart, I'm a patient man. A very patient man."

He continued driving for another mile before making his way over a bumpy, unpaved road. The tall steeple of a small white-shingled church appeared in a clearing of towering pine trees. He maneuvered into the church's parking lot, parking beside Abigail's stately vintage Mercedes.

Cleve gathered his jacket from the rear seat, slipping into it before assisting her from the car. He offered her his arm and they joined the other church members walking from the dusty parking lot to the church.

Rina waited patiently beside Cleve, her hand tucked into the bend of his arm, as he introduced her to people he had known all of his life. They joined Abigail, Darren, Maddie, Rubel and Emily-Jane, who were already seated in a pew that had brass plates engraved with the Whitney name on the armrests. Philip and Carole were missing.

She felt a sense of belonging when she sat beside Cleve in the family pew. His solid, broad shoulder pressed intimately against hers, and she leaned into his strength.

Even sitting in church with Cleve was a different experience for Rina as she found herself comparing Cleve to Jason again. Jason never attended church services, except for weddings or funerals, even though he had been raised in a home where everyone was expected to attend church services every Sunday.

Snapping, hand-held cardboard fans sliced the thick air, punctuating the rising and falling voice of the pastor. Rich hymns and spirituals lifted spirits and enveloped everyone attending Little Zion Baptist Church's Sunday morning worship service.

Cleve proved he was a regular churchgoer when he responded with all of the appropriate responses and sang without the aid of the hymnal. His voice was low, rich and pleasant to the ear.

The worship service ended with a melodious blending of voices from both choir and members with "Take My Hand, Precious Lord."

Everyone filed out of the quaint little building and gathered on the front lawn. Cleve's right arm was a protective band of steel around Rina's waist as they stood exchanging pleasantries with the pastor.

Reverend Percy Owens cradled a worn Bible to his chest as he smiled up at Cleve. The smile smoothed out a network of tiny lines in his ancient face. Earlier Cleve had mentioned to Rina that the pastor had recently celebrated his eighty-ninth birthday.

"Well, Cleveland, you can always count on Little Zion for our support of your candidacy. I can honestly say you're one of Savannah's best. Especially since I've watched you grow up to be a fine young man. I'm going to talk to the deacons," he continued without taking a breath, "and our church sisters about puttin' on somethin' in the next few weeks to do our share so we can put some money in your campaign purse." Pausing, he inhaled deeply. "I don't want folks sayin' we don't take care of our own."

Cleve nodded, appearing genuinely moved by Reverend Owens's offer. "With folks like you and the members of our church, I can't lose." His fingers tightened on Rina's waist. "And I must say I've been truly blessed to have found someone like Rina to join my campaign team."

Reverend Owens, his eyes clouded with advanced age, peered closely at Rina. "I say you've been double blessed, son." He turned slightly when a deacon called out his name. "If you'll excuse me, I must have a word with Deacon Barnes before he leaves." He patted Cleve's arm. "Remember, son, you owe me a wedding. I don't intend to get cheated twice."

Rina felt the punishing grip of Cleve's fingers when the pastor mentioned marriage, wondering when Cleve had been engaged. There had always been talk that Cleveland Whitney never appeared in public with a marriageable woman.

She remembered Abigail mentioning a woman named Paige, and she wondered who Paige was and how involved she had been with Cleve.

"He's charming, Cleve," she remarked as she and Cleve returned to the parking lot.

His grip eased on her slender body. "Reverend Owens has a heart of gold. There isn't anything he wouldn't do for one of God's creatures."

"Including you?" she teased.

He nodded, smiling broadly. "We have the rest of the day before us. What do you want to do?"

She felt the penetrating rays of the hot June sun through the fabric of her linen dress. "I wouldn't mind swimming."

Cleve opened the car door. "We'll go one better, sweetheart. We'll have a picnic on the beach."

Rina slipped onto her seat, smiling up at him. "That sounds wonderful."

CHAPTER 14

Rina stood at the sink in the kitchen at Cleve's house, the knife in her hand poised over the dark green skin of a small round watermelon.

"Do you want me to leave it in slices, or cut it off the rind?"

"It doesn't matter," Cleve replied, stirring a thick mixture of spicy barbecue sauce. He stared at her profile, finding her enchanting. Her hair was piled on top of her head in sensual disarray as curls dipped over her forehead, and a few errant ones had escaped the elastic band and pins, floating down the nape of her neck.

Her swimsuit was a skimpy two-piece, flame-red creation paired with a matching flame calf-length sarong. A softer vermilion red polish covered the toenails of her slender feet. Rina had no way of knowing that nothing mattered to Cleve, except that she was with him. Her presence soothed him, offering a peace he had never experienced.

She cut the watermelon into small bite-size pieces, while he prepared to baste a rack of spareribs. He took the marinated meat to the outdoor grills and within minutes the distinctive aroma of charcoal-broiled meat filled the air.

Rina placed the watermelon in the refrigerator alongside the potato salad and baked chicken she and Cleve had taken from Mrs. Bailey's refrigerator.

Walking into the living room, she was amazed at her own sense of peace. She felt more alive than she had in more than a year. Being alone with Cleve had renewed her; his presence offered her the respite she had sought for so long.

Everything about this house, its history, its contents, was Cleveland Whitney. There was stability, along with a sense of an unending existence, of continuity.

She stared at faded photographs of long-deceased Whitneys lining the mantel over the fireplace, and she wondered if they were watching over the present owner of the converted warehouse. Were they proud of him?

The glass door slid open and Cleve entered the house. He watched Rina examine the photographs of his deceased relatives, seeing her fingers graze the glass over the faded images.

"They would've loved you, Rina," he said reverently. She spun around and he smiled at her. "They would've loved your beauty, your intelligence and your gentle spirit." Crossing the room, he closed the space between them. "Some of the more pompous ones probably would've reluctantly admitted that you're worthy enough to be a Whitney."

Rina placed a small hand over his broad bare chest. Touching his flesh, standing close to him, swept her away in a tidal wave of longing.

Tilting her head, she gave him a long, penetrating look.

"What do you say, Cleve? Am I worthy enough to be a Whitney?"

His hand went to her neck, the thumb grazing the delicate bones along her jaw line. His jet-black eyes blazed into hers. "The question should be, am I worthy of you? You're a queen, Rina. Royalty." Lowering his head, he moved closer.

"Permission requested to kiss you," he murmured above her mouth.

Her arms curved around his strong neck as she rose on tiptoe. "Permission granted," she breathed into his mouth only seconds before he covered hers in a slow, drugging kiss.

His demanding lips caressed hers and Rina opened her mouth, receiving the full force of his passion. His hands eased down her spine to her hips, pulling her to him until she felt the source of his passion, his maleness, searching against her middle. It ended quickly, both of them breathing heavily.

It was only a kiss, but Rina felt as if he had stripped her naked and taken her body.

She walked past him and out of the house, closing the glass door behind her. She stood facing the ocean, reveling in the breeze cooling her fevered flesh.

How easily he aroused her; what she felt with Cleve she had never felt with Jason. She had wanted to be in love with Jason, but she knew she wasn't and had never been.

She knew she was now hopelessly and recklessly in love with Cleveland Whitney.

Cleve speared a small piece of cold melon and extended his fork to Rina. Leaning across the table, she held his thick wrist, guiding the fork to her mouth. Even white teeth closed over the fleshy fruit as she bit into it.

Cleve's dark eyes crinkled in a smile. "Have you eaten your fill, Your Highness?"

Rina collapsed against the cushiony softness of her chair, laughing. It was a game Cleve had played all afternoon; he felt it was his duty to wait on her as if she were truly royalty.

"Yes," she said, holding up a slender hand.

Cleve finished the sliced fruit, chewing thoughtfully while staring at Rina. The hot sun had darkened her skin and lightened her hair until it resembled burnished gold threads entwined in swirls of tortoise-shell curls. The pinpoints of green in her light gray-brown eyes sparkled like precious emeralds.

Rina watched Cleve watching her, feeling like a hapless creature transfixed by a larger predator. She wanted to run, but knew it was useless; she knew he would subdue her and yet there was nothing she could do about it; she was defenseless because unknowingly she had given him the power to take from her what she had always withheld from any man: passion.

But she wondered whether there had been a woman, or women, who had once had all of Cleveland Whitney. Had there been someone he had surrendered to?

"Who's Paige?" she asked without warning. Cleve stared at her, complete surprise on his face, then he recovered quickly.

"Paige Ross is Jimmy Ross's daughter."

Now it was Rina's turn to be surprised. "You are involved with what is now your opponent's daughter?"

He shot her a scowl. "We were not involved. I saw her a few times."

"What's a few times?"

Leaning back on his chair, Cleve managed a hint of a smile. "This is the first time I've ever been cross-examined. And by one so beautiful," he added with a full grin.

"You're impossible," she sputtered. She wanted answers and Cleve was teasing her. Placing her napkin on the table, she stood up. "I'm going for a walk before I swim," she announced, not looking at him.

He rose with her. "May I join you. Your Highness?"

"It's your property and your beach," she countered in a quiet voice.

"And it could be yours," he retorted as quietly.

Rina clamped her teeth tightly. Cleveland Whitney had launched a second campaign, a personal campaign to win her from Jason.

She left the patio and he followed, catching up with her and capturing her hand. He held it gently in his as they walked slowly along the beach, each lost in their private thoughts while the sun played a game of hide and seek behind low cumulus clouds.

She suggested they stop, and both sank down to the sand. She drew her knees up to her chest, cradling her legs with her arms, while Cleve stretched out on his back, muscled arms covering his face.

Rina studied him as he lay motionless. Moments later, she straightened and lay beside him, her face pressed to his hard shoulder. Cleve stirred, shifted on his side and pulled her closer.

Cleveland Graham Whitney was perfect, she thought. He had everything needed to make him successful: name, looks, intelligence, breeding and ambition. And he would make his mark in history as many of his ancestors had done.

"I'm one of the lucky ones, Cleve," Rina whispered.

"Why?" he asked drowsily, close to her lips.

"Because I can honestly say that I'm truly fortunate to have been born during this lifetime and to have known you."

She did not feel the shudder shake Cleve's body as his eyes telegraphed the same desire flowing from hers. Smiling, she curved an arm around his neck. He shifted slightly, bringing her closer and cradling her thigh between his knees.

She felt the heady sensation of his lips against her neck and shoulder. Rina clung to him, trembling with a need that surpassed anything she had ever known.

Cleve positioned her so her back was pressed to the sand. His head dipped and his tongue traced the slight swell of her breasts, which rose above the deep V of her top. It flicked over the tiny dark mole on her right breast.

Her fingers curved under his jaw, forcing his head up. Her mouth searched for his, offering him what she could not deny any longer: her passion, her surrender.

Their tongues met, dueled, then curled around each other in a slow dance of desire.

His hand covered a breast and Rina felt it swell and ache with desire as his demanding mouth caressed hers, searching and powerful.

He called, she came. He asked, she answered. He demanded, she gave.

He slid the straps of her top off her shoulders, his hands slowly, purposefully, relieving her of the garment. His gaze competed with the summer sun as the heat kissed the small, firm gold mounds with their darker brown nipples.

"I want you, darling," he gasped heavily. "I want to be your friend and your lover, Rina."

She knew she could not, would not, stop him. It had passed the point of no return.

"Love me." The two words floated out above her, fading in the soft, hot breeze sweeping the beach.

A volcanic shudder wracked Cleve when he registered her acquiescence.

He curbed his runaway impulse to take her quickly, as he carefully, methodically, untied the flame-red sarong and spread it out beside her on the pale sand. The top to her swimsuit and skimpy bottom followed.

There, on the beach, Rina lay naked, eyes closed, a visual feast for Cleveland Whitney. The blood ran hot in her veins, the desire increasing for the man kneeling above her.

"Cleve…" Whatever Rina was going to utter was drowned in the fire of the kiss burning her mouth. He captured her wrists, holding them to her sides, not permitting her movement, as he moved down the length of her body, branding her his possession.

Passions spiraling out of control, Rina surrendered to Cleveland Whitney. He kissed her mouth, lingered lovingly, achingly, over her breasts and flat abdomen, then brushed his lips over her soft, silky sex that had become a smoldering flame, bringing forth its own sweet and feminine fragrance and moisture.

She clenched and unclenched her teeth and hands. What was happening to her was real, not a dream. The man making love to her was real, not an illusion.

She tried but couldn't stop the lithe whimpers of desire from escaping, and she arched as his tongue swept over the tiny nub hidden with the folds of her femininity. Without warning, the explosions rocked her womb. What started out as small ripples became waves that swelled, shattered until she cried out with the magical force which took her, body and mind, beyond herself, lifting her higher and higher until she was thrust beyond reality.

She returned and Cleve gathered her gently to his chest. Rina could not move or talk. Her heart raced uncontrollably as she clung to him in fright. What had just happened to her was beyond her experience and beyond comprehension.

Her slender fingers spread over the hardness of Cleve's chest, then moved downward. He halted their descent, smiling. "We can't go any further, darling. I can't protect you out here."

She blushed furiously as her love for Cleve swelled within her. He had given her pleasure while selfishly foregoing his own.

Brushing his lips over hers, he said, "I thought we were going for a walk before swimming."

Rina averted her gaze, noting the teasing smile softening his mouth. "It was my intent to swim, Cleve."

"And it was my intent to drown, sweetheart," he replied in a soft tone. "Drown in your body."

He rolled off her body and Rina reached for the minuscule pieces of her swimsuit. Moments later she had rewrapped the sarong around her slender waist, watching Cleve watch her every motion.

And watching him watch her, she again felt the heat of his mouth on her mouth, her breasts, abdomen, thighs and on her pulsing sex. Even without touching her, he had the power to make her quake with desire.

She knew she had been changed the moment he bared her body and claimed the passion she had never offered any man, but she did not know how much he too had been changed by his selfless act of loving and worshipping her body with the majesty of the sky as their canopy and the wonder of sand to cradle their desire.

Both of them had been indelibly changed, forever. Cleve held out both arms, and Rina floated into his embrace. "Let's go home."

And it was back at the converted warehouse that she experienced the full power of Cleve's lovemaking. She reciprocated unselfishly as she learned how to give him as much pleasure as he had given her. She stroked him relentlessly, stopping at the threshold of completion. She felt sensual heat from her toes to her breasts, her entire body tingling in anticipation of fulfillment.

And when she felt as if she would go crazy if he didn't take her, he claimed her body with a strong, smooth thrust of raw possession.

And not once did Rina think of Jason; not until she and Cleve lay motionless, sated, his arms holding her protectively.

"I love making love to you," Cleve said, his breathing normal for the first time. "And I want to make love to you every day. But I know that can't happen until Harper is out of your life."

The blood ran cold in her veins, washing away her ardor like a frigid wave pounding the rocky coastline. She closed her eyes tightly, gold-tipped lashes concealing her turmoil.

"No!"

Cleve moved quickly, looming above her and imprisoning her shoulders between strong fingers. "Do you love him?" Rina caught her lower lip between her teeth, biting down hard enough to draw blood. "Do you love him?" he repeated against her damp face.

She wrestled with her internal anguish. Cleve had ruined an exquisite afternoon of lovemaking when he mentioned Jason Harper. "I don't know," she finally confessed. "So help me, I don't know, Cleve." She didn't see him smile.

His lips brushed hers in a soft, healing motion. "It's going to be all right, sweetheart. As long as you didn't say that you love him, I know it's going to be good between us."

Her hands moved from his shoulders to frame his cheeks. She examined the strong face she had come to love. The fingers of her right hand feathered over his ear, then up to his coarse, tightly curled hair. It was soft and springy to the touch as she massaged the hair on the nape of his neck.

"Will you give me time, Cleve?"

He frowned. "Time for what?"

"I want to work out my relationship with Jason. I can't just walk away from him," she explained.

He pressed a kiss over each eyelid, smiling. "I don't want you to walk away from him, Rina. I want you to search your heart for the truth. It'll give you the right answer."

She returned his smile. "You sound like an expert, Cleveland Whitney."

"At thirty-eight I've learned to be honest with myself, Rina. To lie to oneself usually leads to failure and disappointment."

She sighed, nodding. "I think my heart knows me better than I know myself."

Cleve returned her to the cradle of his embrace. "You're not a quick lay, Rina. You're much more special than that. I was certain of that the moment you placed a narrow foot on Whitney property."

"I thought you were too incensed with my presence to notice anything about me," she retorted with a grin.

"Fishing for a compliment, darling?" he teased, arching his eyebrows.

"Of course not, darling," she returned softly.

"Well, I noticed a lot about you that afternoon, Rina, things I will tell you one of these days. I was prepared to throw everything in my verbal arsenal at you because of Harper's posturing arrogance when he threatened me about you."

She cradled Cleve's head to her breasts. "I'm sorry he threatened you."

"I'm not," he admitted, his voice muffled against her chest. Cleve raised his head. "Harper just reinforced my distaste for him. And when you wouldn't permit me to intimidate you, I knew he wasn't man enough to hold onto you."

"And are you man enough?" she questioned, basking in the knowledge that she was now beyond his intimidation.

He released her, pulling himself up against the bed's headboard. Staring out across the bedroom, he said, "Yes, and you know it," he added with gentle arrogance.

Rina sat up beside him, pulling a sheet up over her naked breasts. "You're right about that," she admitted. "But I also know that I'm woman enough to entice, excite and enthrall the infamous Cleveland Graham Whitney. Has any woman ever done that before?" she asked.

Cleve stared, shocked. Rina had read him as if he were an open book. But she had no way of knowing that not even Paige Ross knew Cleveland Whitney that well.

"It's all right," she crooned. "You don't have to answer the question, Cleve." Lowering her chin, she glanced up at him through her lashes. "Your eyes give you away, darling."

"Touché," he replied softly. "Does it give you a thrill to know that you have that much power over me, Rina Matthews?"

She shook her head. "No, Cleve. It doesn't give me a thrill. It's very comforting to know what I feel for you is reciprocated," she confessed, feeling as if the tight fist around her heart had been released. "You don't know how comforting that is."

"I'll never hurt you…"

"Don't," she urged, placing her fingers over his mouth. "Never say never, Cleve." Her mouth replaced her fingers. "Let's just enjoy what we have."

He crushed her body to his, his hands cupping the slim roundness of her hips. He settled her against the cradle of his maleness, making her more than aware of the power of his desire.

Rina pressed her open mouth to his and there was a sweet intimacy that had not been there before. It was soul-searching and satisfying. The world stopped spinning on its axis as Rina and Cleve offered each other a glimpse of paradise.

In the converted warehouse on the beach, it was perfection, God's perfect creations abounding, and all was right in their private world. Cleve's head came up and he rubbed his thumb over Rina's swollen lips. He gathered her closer, pressing his mouth to her scented hair. Her perfume clung to his flesh, making him a part of her.

She clung to him, her arms curving under his and grasping her shoulders tightly. She was astonished with the sense of fulfillment flowing through her mind and body. A cocoon of contentment surrounded her, and the emotion that passed between them was warm, open and uncomplicated.

But the harder she tried to ignore the truth the more it haunted her: she wanted Cleve to love her, not just her body, but love her for herself, unselfishly, because she loved him unselfishly. She had proven that by offering all of herself. Could she hope he would love her as much as she was in love with him? A shudder wracked her body.

"What's the matter, Rina?" Cleve had felt her shake.

"Hold me, Cleve," she whispered fervently.

"I am, darling," he murmured in her hair.

"Closer, tighter," she pleaded.

He tightened his hold on her slender frame. "What's frightening you, sweetheart?"

Rina raised her head, kissing his throat. "Nothing," she lied. "It's just that I don't want this to be a dream, and when I wake up you'll be gone."

His laugh was low and sensual. "This is real, Rina." He pulled back the sheet, revealing his hardness. "None of this would've ever happened if you hadn't come to Whitney Hall. And now it's too late to back out."

She couldn't pull her gaze away from his magnificent erection. "I'm stuck with you?"

Cleve grinned. "No. We're stuck with each other." He ran a hand over a quivering breast. "Come, let me show you."

And he expertly showed and shared sensual delights that Rina never imagined. Sated, they slept, then showered together, changed clothes, and sat on the patio watching the sun set beyond the horizon, while soft strains of music floated from the house.

Rina thought only about the man sitting beside her and the moment.

CHAPTER 15

A soft, dark velvet surrounded Rina and Cleve as they made their way back to Whitney Hall. What had passed between them that afternoon was still too new to verbalize.

She relied on Cleve's sense of familiarity with the vast property as he led her over hidden foot trails, his fingers tightening protectively on hers whenever they made their way to an overgrown section of landscape.

The night air was redolent with the smell of damp earth and blooming night flowers, and she felt a sense of loss when they stepped through the entry at Whitney Hall. She had not wanted her time with Cleve to end.

An agitated Abigail met Cleve as he escorted Rina across the expanse of the living room. "I called your place, Cleveland, but you must have been on your way here."

He noted his mother was dressed for traveling. She wore a yellow silk dress and black patent leather pumps. "What's the matter, Mother?"

Abigail inhaled deeply to calm herself. "I'm going to Savannah."

"Why tonight, Mother? Can't it wait until tomorrow?" he questioned, a slight frown creasing his forehead.

"No. Madeline needs me. She had an argument with Darren the moment they returned home."

Cleve mumbled a savage expletive under his breath. "Why the hell doesn't she leave him once and for all? Why can't she accept that she made a mistake marrying him?"

Abigail pulled a set of keys from her purse. "She's going to have to work out her problems with her husband by herself, Cleveland. I've cancelled all of my meetings for next week, so I gave Mrs. Bailey the time off." She laid a hand on Rina's arm. "I'm sorry, child, but this can't be avoided."

Rina offered Abigail an understanding smile. "It's all right. If I have any questions, they can wait until you return."

Abigail took in Rina's sun-browned face and brightly streaked hair. She also noted her son's tender expression whenever he glanced at the young woman standing at his side.

"Thank you for understanding, Rina. Cleveland," she began, addressing her eldest child, "I want you to sleep here the nights I'll be away. I don't want Rina and Mrs. Wells here without some male protection."

Cleve gave Rina a sidelong glance. "Don't worry about Rina, Mother. I'll take good care of her."

Abigail nodded, then leaned over and kissed Rina's cheek. "Thank you again."

Cleve gathered his mother to his chest, kissing her mouth. "Please drive carefully."

"I will, darling." She patted his cheek. "I'll call you when I arrive."

"If Maddie needs me, tell her I'll come," he offered.

"No, Cleveland. You know if you get involved it's not going to be nice. Madeline knows better than anyone that her brothers are ready to take her husband apart, limb by limb. Let me try to handle it this time."

"Darren Jackson's luck is going to run out one of these days," Cleve predicted.

"Think of the baby Madeline's carrying, Cleveland," Abigail reminded him. "The baby's a Jackson, but it's also a Whitney." Cleve nodded, even though he was not pleased with his mother's reminder.

Rina stood at the door, watching him walk Abigail to her car. Cleve stared at the red taillights until they disappeared; then he turned and walked back into the house, closing the door and locking it.

His fingers circled Rina's wrist, and he brought her hand to his mouth, kissing each finger before his tongue flicked over her palm.

She wanted to pull her hand away, but didn't. The feathering sensations floating up and down her arm were too pleasurable, too intoxicating.

The golden light from twin lamps highlighted his smiling mouth. "Do you think you can put up with me for a week?" he teased.

"Can we put up with each other for a week?" she asked, answering his question with one of her own.

"Only time will tell, Rina," he replied, leading her back into the living room.

"You don't appear too fond of your brother-in-law," she remarked, as they climbed the curving staircase.

"He's wrong for Maddie."

"Other than his age, he appears charming enough for her," Rina said, noting Cleve's frown.

"I can put up with his being twenty years older than my sister, but I can't put up with his lack of initiative or ambition. The man comes from a good family, he's well traveled and very, very talented. Darren is a virtuoso pianist. He was hailed as a prodigy by the time he turned ten."

"Does he still play?" she asked, as they walked down the hail and neared their bedrooms.

"No. He's too content to sleep late and then waste the rest of the day sipping bourbon cocktails. All that's missing is someone fanning the sweat from his brow while he lounges on the veranda," Cleve spat out contemptuously.

"Maybe you're being a little too hard on him, Cleve."

"I'm not hard enough. But the only nice thing can say about Darren Jackson is that he loves my sister, and that he's faithful to her. The man's too lazy to even contemplate having an extramarital affair."

Rina laughed at his dour expression. 'They'll work it out, Cleve. Especially if they love each other."

Cleve stopped at the door to Rina's room and stared down at her. She appeared more delicate and ethereal than he had ever seen her before.

"Perhaps you're right," he agreed.

Rina touched his arm and kissed his jaw. "Good night, Cleve."

Leaning down, he kissed the tip of her nose. "Good night, love."

She opened the door and stepped into her room. The powerful scent of roses filled her nostrils, and the glow from the bedside lamp revealed the single bud on her pillow.

Placing the flower in the vase with the others, she walked over to the French doors. Opening them, she stepped out onto the veranda.

She folded her body down to a cushioned chair and stared out into the night. She tried identifying the constellations in the summer sky, smiling when she located a few.

She sat for hours, thinking of Jason and her feelings for him. She thought about her own dreams and aspirations; she thought about the plans she had made for her future and suddenly it became very clear to her. She could have a future with Jason, but not as his wife. Not after making love to Cleve.

The light from the adjoining bedroom went out, leaving the far end of the veranda in complete darkness. Cleve had gone to bed, and Rina knew it was time for her to go to her own bed.

She reentered her bedroom, stripped off her clothes and slipped nude between the cool, clean sheets.

I'll follow my heart, she thought, and with that she slept soundly throughout the night.

Rina felt the warming rays of the sun on the side of her face as she sat in the large comfortable armchair in her office. She had been up before dawn, rewriting her notes for a proposal.

She had been able to ascertain the bottom line figure on Abigail's personal wealth, but the numbers did not include the widow's interests in the enterprises controlled and operated by her sons. Abigail and Rubel owned controlling shares in two radio stations, while she shared equal control with Philip in a Savannah news weekly. Nothing indicated her involvement with Cleve or Maddie. Had Abigail's oldest son and her only daughter elected not to become involved with their family's business holdings? Or for reasons unknown had the two been disinherited?

There was a slight tap on the door and she started. "Come in."

The door swung open, and Cleve pushed a serving cart filled with covered dishes and china into the room. His gaze swept over Rina's body, then settled on her flushed face.

"Good morning, Cleve." Her voice was low and breathless.

His smile was slow in coming. "Good morning, Rina." He removed a white tablecloth from the lower shelf of the cart and spread it out over a table. She watched as he quickly and expertly set the table with china and silver.

Rina silently assessed his masculine physique in a pair of light gray slacks and an off-white, pullover V-neck sweater. This morning he had foregone his usual shorts and casual shirts.

"Mother asked that I make certain you take your meals," he announced. "She says you don't eat enough."

Her eyes crinkled in laughter as she rose to her feet. "I've eaten more this past week than I've eaten in all of last month. And if I gain too much weight I won't be able to fit into the dress I bought for the ball."

He raised expressive eyebrows, staring at her. "Do you have a date for the ball?"

She gave him a sassy smile. "Not yet."

An equally sensual smile curved Cleve's full mouth. "You still have some time."

Rina felt his pull from across the room, his charm and his overwhelming male virility.

"Will you save a dance for me, Rina?" His gaze narrowed as he surveyed her hair tumbling in provocative disarray around her face. It was still damp from her morning shower.

"For you I'll save two," she promised him.

He nodded slowly. "I'm going to hold you to that promise."

"And I never renege on a promise."

He nodded again. "What color is your dress?"

"Black with white seed pearls." She moved to the table, watching Cleve uncover a dish filled with hash brown potatoes and another with fluffy omelets.

He smiled. "You compromised."

"I was told it's a one-of-a-kind creation. I didn't want to see myself in something I'd picked off a department store rack."

Pulling out a chair, Cleve seated Rina, curbing the impulse to pull her into his arms and kiss her until she was breathless, intoxicated with the passion she aroused in him.

"You women worry about not being seen wearing the same dress, while all men manage to look like either penguins or waiters. There isn't too much one can do with a tuxedo or a dinner jacket."

Rina smiled at Cleve when he sat down opposite her. "But not all men look the same in their tuxedos or dinner jackets."

"You're right about that," he conceded, pouring steaming coffee into translucent, fragile china cups.

"But back to your gaining some weight. You could use a few extra pounds."

She folded her hands on her hips. "Are you saying I'm skinny?"

"Not at all," he replied. "Remember, sweetheart, I've seen you without your clothes." This brought a wave of color to her face. "However, you could use some filling out in a few areas."

Her mouth gaped in utter astonishment. "How can you fix your mouth to be so insulting, Cleveland Whitney!"

He shrugged broad shoulders under the V-neck sweater.

"Not insulting, Rina. Honest. You're so used to men fawning over you that you ignore the truth. You're a beautiful woman and you're well aware of that. But you're also like a tightly closed bud. With time, love and infinite patience you'll open slowly to blossom and reveal your inner beauty. I glimpsed a portion of that yesterday. And that beauty will never fade, darling. I've also noticed that you're tired, drained. There are times when you're so tense that I'm afraid of saying anything to you. You work too hard, don't get enough sleep and you don't eat regularly."

Rina felt the heat in her face. Just because he had made love to her he had no right to lecture her. "What do you prescribe, Dr. Feelgood?"

"I suggest you learn to live, Rina," he countered. "Take time to smell the flowers. They'll be here longer than you or me."

She filled her plate with an omelet, hash browns and a slice of golden-brown toast. "I have a business to run, Cleve."

"A business that could probably run itself."

"I doubt that," she argued softly.

Cleve stared at her. "If you're that doubtful, why did you consent to take my mother's account?"

Rina lowered her gaze. "I didn't feel that way before accepting the assignment."

"Why now, Rina?"

How could she tell Cleve that Jason hadn't followed through with his responsibility of managing the day-to-day activities of the office? That he had overdrawn their account? That he was spending money without first consulting her?

He stabbed his omelet with his fork. "It's Harper, isn't it?" he asked perceptively.

She nodded, staring down at the food on her plate. "I'm going to have to talk to Jason. Especially now that the firm will be responsible for your campaign finances."

Cleve's jaw hardened as he stared at her bowed head. "You can't do it all, Rina. I pressured you into accepting the position of handling my election finances, but be damned if I'll let you burn yourself out trying to cover Harper's butt."

Her head came up quickly. "I'll handle my partner, thank you." She had said the same thing to the manager of the bank in Atlanta.

"Can you, Rina?" Cleve asked in a dangerously soft tone.

She lifted her chin. "I have so far."

"I'm not Abigail Whitney," he reminded her. "My mother is a very forgiving person."

"And you're not?"

"Not when people screw up, Rina."

She glared at him. "I'm not going to screw up, Cleve."

He returned her glare. "Just make certain Harper doesn't."

Again, the topic of Jason Harper had come up like a poisonous viper, rearing its ugly head to drive a wedge between her and Cleve.

After a lengthy silence, Cleve said, "I have to go to Savannah to sign some papers. I'd like you to come with me."

His invitation to go with him to Savannah was totally unexpected. "I can't, Cleve," she replied. "My computer is scheduled for delivery today." His impassive expression did not change.

"What time do you expect it to be delivered?"

"Anytime between nine and five."

His features settled into a deep frown. "I don't like leaving you here alone."

"I won't be alone," she countered. "Mrs. Wells will be here."

"I suppose you're right," he murmured to himself.

Cleve waited for Rina to finish her breakfast, then cleared the table, placing the soiled dishes and silver on the cart.

"We'll eat out tonight," he stated firmly.

Rina put her hands together and bowed her head. "Yes, master." His eyes crinkled in amusement as he studied her submissive posture. "Something else, master?"

"I want you to grant me one wish," he crooned in a tone as fluid as flowing silk.

She dropped her hands, her head coming up. His gaze devoured her, leaving no doubt as to what he wanted.

"I can't, master. It's the genie's day off," she said innocently.

Cleve threw back his head, laughter erupting from his throat. "Coward!" he taunted. "Tease," he continued, pushing the cart across the room. "Ninny," he threw over his shoulder before he closed the door.

You're the tease, Cleve, Rina thought. Just being who he was taunted her relentlessly night and day.

The phone rang, startling her, and she moved over to the desk to answer it.

"Rina Matthews."

"Good morning, baby," crooned a familiar male voice.

Her nerves screamed. "I'm not your damned baby. So cut it out, Jason!"

Jason chuckled. "Calm down, Rina. We should be celebrating instead of fighting. I couldn't believe the news when I got in last night and heard that we'd managed to get a piece of the Whitney campaign. You must have really worked your show with Cleveland."

"I had nothing to do with it, Jason. Cleve needed a finance manager and I just happened to be available." Her voice was a flat monotone.

"Nonetheless, it looks as if we're on a roll."

A slight frown touched Rina's forehead. "What are you talking about?"

"Garritson has arranged for me to meet with some of his business associates. They want to set up a consortium."

She did not feel the joy she should have felt when she registered Jason's statement. It was something she had wanted from the first time she formed a business alliance with Jason Harper. Thomas Garritson was one of Atlanta's most successful businessmen.

"I'm going to be out of the office for the next five days, Rina," Jason informed her. "Garritson and his people have set up around-the-clock meetings so we can put the deal to bed as quickly as possible."

"You're not going to be in the office." It was a statement, not a question.

"I have no choice, Rina." Jason's voice had also hardened. "I'll monitor the office by telephone."

"So will I," she retorted between clenched teeth. "When can we meet?"

"When, Rina?" He sensed the coldness in her tone.

"Yes, Jason, when? You and I have to talk—in person."

There was a pause. "How about next Monday?"

"Fine," she replied. "Meet me in Savannah."

"Where and at what time?"

"Make it three o'clock at the Palm Garden."

"Okay, Rina. The Palm Garden at three," he repeated.

They exchanged further polite pleasantries, then hung up.

Rina felt like a robot, reacting without any emotion. It was as if all of her feelings for Jason had evaporated like a wisp of smoke.

Meeting with Jason would signal a beginning and an end, and she prayed it would go smoothly.

CHAPTER 16

The amber figures were lined up in columns on the screen like rows of ants. Rina had spent the better part of three hours entering figures from the spreadsheets. She went through several functions, then pushed a key. Within seconds printed pages emerged from the laser printer. Entering the numbers into the computer saved needless hours of manual computation.

Raising her arms above her head, she flexed her shoulders and rotated her head in a circular motion.

"New dance, Rina?"

Her arms came down and she swiveled on the chair. Cleve stood in the doorway, watching her antics. "No," she answered, smiling. "I'm trying to get the kinks out of my neck," she explained, massaging the back of her neck.

"Here, let me do that." He walked over and stood behind her. His large hands grazed the column of her neck, his fingers inching slowly over her collarbone. His thumbs pressed against the top of her spine, applying pressure and making her wince.

"Relax, sweetheart," he urged softly against her cheek. "I won't hurt you."

She obeyed, giving into the strength of his warm hands on her flesh. The narrow straps of her dress exposed her neck and shoulders.

Closing her eyes, Rina floated beyond herself. His touch was impersonal, yet there was something about the way his long fingers curved around the base of her throat that brought back images of their lovemaking the day before.

She moaned slightly as he kneaded the heel of his hand along the length of her spine. "That's good," she moaned.

"You're very tight, Rina. You're like a bow ready to snap with the slightest tug."

"Too much concentration," she gasped, her breath hissing through her teeth.

"Am I hurting you, darling?"

"No." He wasn't hurting her, but all of her senses were heightened by his erotic ministrations, the heat from his body, the distinctive masculine scent that was only his, and the soothing, healing touch of his fingers on her bare skin.

Cleve leaned closer, his tips touching her hair.

"The next time you need a massage we'll do it the right way. I'll heat some oil and rub it all over your body." She stiffened under his touch and he chuckled wickedly, "Don't worry, Rina. I won't attack you."

Turning her head, she glanced up at him. "I'm not worried about you attacking me." It was the thought of him rubbing oil on her naked body that affected her.

He released her, sitting down on the corner of the desk. He watched a myriad of emotions cross her face. "I told you before that I would never take what you're not willing to give me, Rina. And that means everything. If you don't want me to make love to you, I won't. If you don't want me to kiss you, I won't. And if you don't want me to touch you, I won't."

What did he expect her to say? That what she felt for him went beyond a casual liking? That she did not know where liking ended and loving began? That for the first time she doubted whether she could spend the summer at Whitney Hall without blurting out that she loved him?

She smiled. "I appreciate your honesty, Cleve."

"I don't want your appreciation," he countered quickly.

A slight frown furrowed her smooth forehead. "What is it you want?"

He traced the curve of her cheek and jaw with a finger. Then, without warning, both hands cupped her face, pulling her up gently from her chair. She stood in front of him, staring into the fathomless depths of his dark eyes. A sensuous light passed between them as his gaze searched her face, her heart.

"Don't you know, darling?" he asked so softly that she had to strain to hear what he was saying.

A brief shudder rippled through Rina as she stood motionless, only the throbbing pulse in her throat indicating she was alive and warm to the touch.

Cleve's eyes widened as he took in her brilliant orbs, washed with pinpoints of green and gold.

"Don't you know?" he repeated.

"You want to make love to me," she replied trance-like.

He froze, his feature contorted in shock. "Is that what you think?"

Rina tried nodding, but failed when his fingers tightened ground her jaw. "Yes," she mumbled.

He stood up, towering above her like an avenging giant. 'For all of your intelligence, you're pretty naive, Rina. Why should I want you for sex when I could sleep with a dozen other women?"

Her face burned against his fingers. "Then why don't you just do that!"

His hands dropped and he pushed them into the pockets of his slacks. He turned away rather than let her witness his full-blown anger. "Don't ever tell me who to sleep with, Rina."

Her jaw dropped. "I-I didn't tell you who to sleep with."

He turned back to her, lips thinning. "And don't play word games with me. You can't possibly hope to win."

Her temper rose, meeting his. "And don't you dare try to put words in my mouth, Cleveland Graham Whitney. I know what I said."

"How do you know what you've said when you don't even know what you want?"

He started to walk away, but Rina reached out, catching the front of his sweater. "What's that supposed to mean?"

He rounded on her. "Anything you want it to mean. Now, will you please let go of my sweater." She released it, and he glanced down at the stretched-out cotton and silk knit material. "It looks as if I'm deformed, Rina."

She stared at the unsightly fullness of the fabric over his right breast. Her hand shot out, pulling the left side and achieving an equal fullness. "Now you have a matched pair, Mr. Whitney."

Cleve blinked unbelievingly. It looked as if he had miraculously acquired a pair of rounded breasts. His anger vanished when he saw Rina's lips twitch in amusement. He ran a hand over his close-cut hair, shaking his head.

"I can't believe this," he whispered. "You've deliberately ruined my sweater." His gaze narrowed. "It happens to be my favorite sweater, Miss Matthews."

She patted his chest, trying to correct the damage. "You earn a decent salary, Cleve. You should be able to buy another one."

He captured her wrist, bringing her up against his body. "I'm on leave and that means I'm not collecting a paycheck."

"Borrow the money from your mother," she suggested.

He increased the pressure on her wrist. It was tight, but not enough to hurt her or leave bruises. "I stopped asking my mother for money when I turned eighteen.

And that means I want you to pay for the damage to my sweater."

"How much did it cost? I'll give you a hundred dollars and we'll call it even."

Cleve ran his tongue over his lower lip, exhibiting a sinister grin. "I don't want your money, sweetheart."

"Just what do you want?" she asked flippantly.

He noted defiance as she tilted her chin. "I want you to marry me, Rina."

She felt her heart stop, then resume beating. "What!"

He gave her a slight shake. "You heard me right the first time, Rina Matthews."

Her eyes grew large and round in her face, while her heart beat wildly under her breasts. All of her instincts indicated that Cleve was serious; it had progressed beyond a game.

She quickly regained control of her runaway emotions.

He pulled her closer. She felt every muscle and hard line of his tall male physique; she also felt the power of his masterful personality and the strength of his maleness searching and sing them together where they had become one.

His impassive expression did not change with her refusal. "Why not?"

"It should be obvious, Cleve."

His eyebrow arched. "It isn't to me, Rina."

"Just because we've slept together doesn't mean that I know you or you know me."

"We'll never know each of her even if we sleep together for fifty years," he argued. "There will always be a part of us that the other will never know or see."

"I…we don't love each other."

"Love will come with time," he retorted, his voice softening and deepening as he smiled. "You've considered marrying Harper, yet you don't know whether you love him."

Rina digested Cleve's argument, believing and not believing. It was as if she wanted everything to be true—to make it easier for her to accept the bold, reckless desire she felt whenever she thought of Cleve.

She stared at his strong throat, watching the slowly beating pulse. She felt his gaze on her lowered head, x-raying her thoughts and reactions.

"Why do you want to marry me, Cleve?"

His arms curved around her waist, holding her gently, protectively. "I want to save you, Rina."

"Save me from what?" His breath was hot against her forehead.

"From Harper and yourself?"

She looked up. "Why? How?"

He pulled her down with him, and she sat on his lap as he laced his fingers together over her flat belly.

"Harper is draining you, darling. Jason Harper is a taker. He only gives when it can benefit him. I realized that the first time I met him years ago, so I doubt whether he loves you, Rina. He may mouth all of the right phrases, but they're only empty words."

Rina stared at the well-groomed hands pressed intimately to her middle. "Why should that matter to you?"

"It matters because I care about you, Rina."

"Why should you care about a stranger, Cleve? And that's what I am to you. An intimate stranger."

"That doesn't matter," he argued.

"It matters to me." Her voice was low and very soft.

"I'll offer to buy out your share of your partnership," he continued as if she hadn't spoken. "I'll set you up with an office in Savannah and…"

"Stop it, Cleve." She tried to break free of his iron grip, and failed.

"I'll offer Harper an amount he can't refuse."

She felt a surge of anger. "You will not. I'm not going to permit you to auction me like a parcel of an estate."

"As Rina Whitney you'll have all of the clout you'll need in Savannah's business and social circles."

She knew she couldn't argue with Cleve, so she tried another approach. "You buy out my share, I marry you, then what, Cleve? Do we negotiate our marriage like a business arrangement? Will it all be on paper?"

He released her waist, turning her around and cupping her face between his palms. Seeing his expression she had her answer before he spoke. "No. If you share my name you'll also share my life and my bed."

She was chilled, numbed by his cold proposal. He hated Jason so much that he was willing to do anything to defeat the man.

"I'm waiting, Rina," he drawled in a bored tone.

"You'll have to wait a long time, mister. The answer is no. I am not available for a hostile takeover at the present time. Or, for that matter, at any time, counselor."

Cleve's eyes were serenely compelling when he smiled down at her flushed face. "I can understand your surprise…"

"Surprise, Cleveland!" she cut in. "It's more like shock."

"I can understand your shock," he corrected, "but the notion also surprised me. I hadn't anticipated asking you to marry me." His hands fell away from her face. "I've said it, and I can't retract my words, because as of this moment I do want to marry you."

Rina felt less threatened now that he wasn't holding her. "Are you usually this impulsive?"

He crossed his arms over his chest. "No." A smile crinkled his eyes.

"Then this too shall pass."

His smile faded. "No, it won't, Rina. I'll ask you again. And I'll keep asking until you give in."

Rina had secretly acknowledged her growing love for Cleve, but in no way would she permit him to use her. Not for himself and not for his scheme to best Jason because he didn't like the man.

"Can't we change this topic, Cleve? It's beginning to wear on my nerves."

Cleve shrugged his shoulders, rising to his feet. "Anything you want," he conceded quickly, glancing down at his watch. "It's time to begin to get dressed for dinner."

Her delicate jaw dropped slightly. He had asked her to marry him, then dismissed it like taking off a tie because it didn't complement what he was wearing.

He had only given her a brief glimpse of his emotions; they ran deep when it came to passion, but she wondered if he was capable of loving a woman. And if she grew to love Cleveland Whitney enough to accept his proposal of marriage, how soon after the ceremony would the passion end, leaving her empty and wanting?

She knew she had given him the right answer. She could not marry a man who did not love her. Whatever love she felt for Cleve she would keep to herself. It would remain her secret.

"Where are we going?" she asked once she recovered.

"There's a private party for a friend of mine at The Crab Shack."

"How formal?"

"Very informal," He gave her a half-smile. "We have to be there by seven-thirty. The party is a surprise."

She returned his smile. "I'll be ready."

Rina and Cleve were conspicuously silent during the drive to The Crab Shack. It was as if too much had been said earlier that afternoon. Both were too cautious to test the other's emotions.

Her casual attire was a white organdy man-tailored shirt and a short black skirt that showed a great deal of long, tanned legs. At the last moment she exchanged her black patent flats for a pair of black patent heels. She had misted her hair and picked out the curls with her fingers, leaving it to dry and frame her small face. It floated around her shoulders like the multi-colored mane of a golden lioness.

Cleve parked the car and came around to help her out, his gaze lingering leisurely on her thighs, knees and legs before offering his hand.

"Too casual, darling?" she asked, knowing he was uneasy about her revealing skirt.

His left arm went around her tiny waist, pulling her to his side. "Not enough skirt, darling," he hissed in her ear.

"It's the latest rage." Her expression was the epitome of innocence.

Cleve's fingers moved up under her breasts. She had not worn a bra, but a white satin and lace camisole took its place. She inhaled sharply as his hand inched up.

"It's trouble, Rina," he warned.

She leaned into him. "Can you handle it, Cleveland?"

He registered her teasing tone and the seductive gleam in her eyes. "Watch me," he challenged.

Rina pulled his hand down and curved her arm through his, smiling up at him as they walked to the entrance of The Crab Shack. The restaurant's parking lot was nearly filled to capacity with late-model luxury automobiles.

Dewey Dixon greeted the arrivals with a wide grin, a handshake for the men and a kiss on the cheek for the women. His eyes twinkled in recognition when he spied Rina on Cleve's arm.

"Welcome back, Rina. It's nice seeing you again." Dewey pressed a friendly kiss to her cheek, then turned his attention to Cleve. "Congratulations, Whit. You've got my vote, brother."

Cleve shook Dewey's hand, pumping it like the politician he soon would become. "Thanks, Dewey."

Dewey's smile faded, his bespectacled eyes shifting from Cleve to Rina and back again to Cleve. "I just thought I'd tell you that Paige is here."

Rina felt the muscles in Cleve's forearm tighten under the fabric of his wheat-colored jacket. She did not look at him, avoiding what she did not want to see—perhaps a remnant of love or desire for another woman.

"Thanks, Dewey." Cleve's voice was low and even, revealing nothing.

Cleve led Rina into the large room that was already filled with people standing around holding drinks and talking quietly. There was an overt lull in conversation as everyone's attention was directed to the newly-arrived couple. Rina felt like a specimen on a slide as dozens of eyes examined her. Unconsciously, she moved closer to Cleve. He covered her hand in the bend of his arm.

"I'm usually not seen in public with a single woman," he said quietly. "Do you think you can handle the gossip?"

Rina tilted her chin, giving him a look of defiance and arrogance. "Watch me," she replied softly.

"I doubt whether I'll be able to watch anyone else tonight."

She had her answer about Paige. Cleve seemed totally unaffected by the announcement of Paige Ross's presence.

She tugged at his arm. "Let's circulate, Cleve. It's not too early for you to begin wooing voters."

Rina thought it was because she was Cleve's date that she garnered everyone's rapt attention. She was unaware that the sun-streaked curling hair sweeping over her shoulders and her very long tanned legs that seemed to go on endlessly from under the short-fitted skirt were the focus of admiring male and envious female gazes.

Paige Ross extracted herself from her adoring date and made her way across the room. Rina had time to assess the woman who could have been Mrs. Cleveland Whitney as she draped her lithe body over Cleve's, kissing him fully on the mouth.

"I've missed you, love," she crooned in a sexy low voice.

Only Cleve's eyes moved as he surveyed her expertly applied makeup. Paige's hair was pulled back in a tight chignon, which accentuated the sculptured beauty of her delicate features in her mahogany-brown face. Her slender figure made Paige appear much taller than her deceptive five-foot, three-inch frame.

"How are you, Paige?" Cleve asked.

Paige did not seem to notice the coldness in Cleve's tone when she linked her arm through his free one. "I'm managing to survive without you, love." Leaning forward, she peered at Rina. "Aren't you going to introduce me to your friend, Cleveland?"

He gently removed Paige's arm. "Paige, this is Rina Matthews. Her company will be responsible for handling my campaign finances. Rina, Paige Ross."

A frown marred Paige's beautiful face. "Must you talk about politics? You know I hate politics, love."

"Paige's father is the mayor of Savannah," he stated, deliberately ignoring Paige's plea that he not talk about politics.

"And your lover hopes to become the next mayor!" Paige shouted.

Rina reacted as if she had been shot. Paige's voice was strident, hysterical. Heads turned in their direction.

Cleve motioned to Paige's date. "Don't you know enough by now not to let her have anything to drink? Get her the hell out of here before she embarrasses herself and her father," he ordered the young man in a low, angry voice.

Rina watched in horror as Paige sagged against her date, sobbing. He swept her up into his arms and carried her through the startled crowd and out of the restaurant.

There was a stilted silence before the guests began talking again. Cleve held Rina's hand tightly, their gazes meeting. A silent plea for understanding went to her. A knowing smile played around the corners of her mouth as she nodded.

"You were very kind to her," she said quietly.

"Paige needs help, darling. Help I can't give her."

"But she's so sad, Cleve."

"She's part of my past and therefore not my responsibility." His tight expression relaxed. "Now I must concentrate on my future, Rina."

Rina accepted a glass of champagne from a passing waiter, handed it to Cleve, then took one for herself. "I'd like to propose a toast." She touched her glass to his. "To Cleveland. May you secure everything you want for your future."

The overhead Tiffany fixtures illuminated Rina in a flood of golden light. Cleve stared deeply into her brilliant green-gray eyes, seeing what Rina would have never said. He watched her put the fluted glass to her mouth. Her seductive crimson lip color became a beacon, beckoning him to taste the honeyed sweetness of her mouth.

"You are my future, Rina," he declared, watching her eyes widen until he saw the dark gray irises dilate and fuse with amber brown. Her hand trembled as she lowered her glass.

Long lashes swept down and touched sculpted cheekbones.

His left hand went to her chin, tilting her face to his. "Yes, Rina."

"Is this a private party, or can anyone join?"

Rina and Cleve, caught up in their own private sensual exchange, forgot they shared a room with some sixty other invited guests.

Cleve managed to drag his gaze away from Rina's face. He smiled warmly. "I don't see why not, Matt. After all, this is your party."

The man Cleve had addressed as Matt shook his hand, but all of his attention was directed toward Rina.

"I knew I could never trust you from the day we met," Matt said to Cleve. "You told me it would be just the two of us for dinner, not half of Savannah."

Cleve clapped a hand on Matt's back. "There was no way I was going to allow you to slip out of town without saying good-bye to everyone." He had not missed Matt's bold perusal of Rina. "Matt, this is Rina Matthews. Rina, Matthew Sterling."

She held out a slender hand, staring up at Matt. He grasped her hand and pressed cool lips to her knuckles. "My pleasure, Rina."

"And mine," she replied, smiling up at the tall man.

Matt Sterling was black and brown velvet with warm, sparkling citrines. The blackness of his hair, the sun-browned darkness of his skin and his remarkable golden eyes reminded her of a big cat—a cheetah. And little did she know that the man was a large, powerful, and often dangerous male predator.

Closing his eyes, Matt sniffed the air. "You're wearing a fragrance made up of myrtle, rose, clove, cardamom and coriander." He leaned closer to Rina. "There's also the slightest hint of patchouli and amber." He smiled a sensual smile. "Did you know that patchouli is considered a love potion?"

Rina stared at him, stunned by his uncanny sense of smell. "It's called Gem."

"And that you are," Matt replied. "A rare and flawless gem. Cleveland is a very lucky man. Now, if you'll excuse me I must circulate with my other guests." He winked at Cleve. "But you two must come and visit before I leave." He released Rina's hand and walked away.

"Where is he going'?" she asked Cleve.

"Matt has bought into a hotel in Mexico City." She looped her free arm through Cleve's.

"Does he live in Savannah?"

"No, darling. He rents a place on St. Simon's Island, but he does most of his socializing in Savannah." Lowering his chin, he dropped a light kiss on the top of her head. "Do you think you'll be able to pull yourself away from your numbers long enough to enjoy an outing on the island?"

Rina flicked her tongue over her lower lip, drawing Cleve's dark gaze to her mouth. "I think I can."

His smile was dazzling. "Good."

That was the last word they exchanged for the next two hours. Rina joined a group of young women who discussed their professions, husbands, children and boyfriends, while Cleve gathered an audience who wanted to hear his plans for the upcoming election.

The large groups divided into smaller ones, then into couples when the band started to play. A man caught Rina's hand, leading her to the dance floor, but he was thwarted when Cleve wove his way through the crowd toward them.

"Sorry, Bobby, but Rina's with me."

"I'm not taking her home, Whit," Bobby explained with a friendly grin. "I just want to dance with the lady."

"You can dance with her later."

Bobby, recognizing the right of territorial possession, released Rina's hand. "No problem, Whit," he conceded.

Cleve swung Rina into a close embrace. "Damn moocher," he grumbled in her ear.

She registered his frown. "All he wanted to do was dance with me."

"Let him dance with his own woman. He does have a woman, Rina," Cleve confirmed. He tightened his hold on her waist, bringing her close enough for their thighs to touch.

In her heels, Rina's head fit perfectly in the hollow between Cleve's shoulder and neck. Her arms went from his shoulders to his neck, and she sank into the warmth of his body. They floated together, moved together, each motion smooth and fluid as if the music had been choreographed just for them and them alone.

Unspoken whispers and desires raced back and forth, telegraphing a savage hunger, a desperate need. Their bodies were in perfect harmony. She needed and he fed her; the desire to share her body with Cleveland Whitney surpassed all reason and common sense.

But at that moment common sense was what Rina lacked most. She wanted to experience the waves of ecstasy he had given her the day before; she wanted the peace Cleve offered, and in turn she would give him the love he sought from a woman.

The musical selection ended and Cleve led Rina through the throng. The next number was a rocking, upbeat tempo which got everyone to their feet, moving in time to the pounding, driving rhythm.

Cleve caught Dewey's arm. "I'll sign the check now."

"You're leaving?" Dewey asked.

Cleve nodded, and Rina was as surprised as Dewey. He handed Cleve a sheet of paper, and Cleve scrawled his signature with a flourish.

"Give them whatever they want," he informed Dewey.

Rina then realized Cleve was underwriting the expense of Matthew Sterling's farewell bash.

"You're very generous," she remarked, once they were seated in his car.

"How's that?"

"Do you usually pick up the tab for your friends' parties?"

Cleve backed out of the parking lot. "It depends on the friend. Matt and I attended the same college and we became very good friends."

"He doesn't sound as if he's from Georgia," she said perceptively.

Cleve smiled and nodded, giving her a quick glance. "That's because he's from Texas. We both were political science majors at George Washington U."

Rina settled back in her seat, turning her face into the warm air floating in through the open window. "Why did we leave so early, Cleve?" She missed the tightening of his jaw.

"I paid my respects and the bill. I didn't think I was obligated to spend the night."

Her head swung around, and she made out his distinctive profile in the dim lights of the dashboard. "You didn't ask me whether I wanted to stay."

"It was either stay and lose a few friends, or leave."

Cleve Whitney was talking in circles again. "Why would you lose friends?"

His right foot floored the accelerator, and the powerful sports car shot forward in a burst of speed over the narrow, unpaved road. "I didn't want to punch out a few of the guys who were ogling you, Rina."

She stifled a laugh. "No one was ogling me."

"They were ogling you," he repeated.

She stared at him, her heart racing with excitement. Could she hope he cared more than he was willing to admit?

He gave her a sidelong glance, taking in her startled expression. "Yes, Rina. I was jealous, is that what you wanted to hear?"

"No." The single word was whispered.

His fingers gripped the steering wheel savagely. "Well, I am," he admitted. "I'm jealous, crazy and as horny as a teenage boy. And I want you in a way that I've never wanted another woman."

Rina inched closer to the door, wanting to disappear. She was totally unprepared for his raw confession.

"Cat got your tongue for a change?" he taunted. "What did you want, Rina? Words of love? Little verses of poetry and flowers? I've managed the flower scene, but everything else fell apart after that.

"Somewhere between putting flowers on your pillow and kissing you Saturday I lost it. Even though the house was filled with family and strangers I still wanted to make love to you—right there. That's how little self-control I have whenever I'm with you."

She turned back to him. "Cleve." She touched his arm, but he jerked away from her.

"Please let me finish, Rina. I want to marry you. I want to lie with you every night. And I want you to have my children. No other woman has ever made me feel this way."

Her mind was a cauldron of hope and fear. "Does it matter to you that I might marry Jason?" She said this, praying Cleve would reveal that he wanted her for herself and not for revenge.

"No more than it mattered when my father met my mother at her first black and white ball. The only difference was Mother was wearing another man's ring and you're not."

Rina couldn't help but smile. "Like father, like son."

"Not quite. Dad had it a lot easier. Mother is a cream puff and you're…"

"I'm what, Cleve?" she asked when his words trailed off.

"You're too damn stubborn and independent for your own good, Rina."

And I love you, she thought.

But she did not feel secure enough to tell him. There was still the nagging problem of her relationship with Jason and their business arrangement; and most of all she still did not feel comfortable knowing Cleve had not released his resentment of Jason.

Yes, he wanted to marry her, but he had not said anything about love; more importantly, Rina knew she could never marry a man who did not return her love.

They returned to Whitney Hall and she climbed the staircase alone, while Cleve stood at the bottom watching her until she made her way down the hall and disappeared into her room.

She closed the door and kicked off her shoes. The night had ended early, yet it was filled with startling revelations. Enough to give her a night of fitful, restless sleep.

CHAPTER 17

Rina reached for the ringing telephone, her gaze still fixed on the printout of a profit and loss statement.

"Rina Matthews." Her attention was momentarily diverted as Bill Newton read a listing of checks Jason had signed for payment.

She wrote down a column of numbers, circling one as a frown creased her forehead. "Are you certain about the amount to the florist?" At first she thought the bank manager had given her an inflated figure.

"I'm positive, Rina," Bill confirmed.

Sighing heavily, she said, "Pay them all." She thanked Bill and rang off.

She then flipped open a leather-bound binder, searching for the number to the florist Harper and Matthews used for plants and gifts for the office and clients.

Her call to the owner of The Golden Stem was more startling and revealing than the one from Bill Newton.

She hung up, experiencing a sense of calm she hadn't thought she possessed. She could not deny the evidence any longer. A triumphant smile parted her lips. The call from Bill Newton had come just in time, because she was to meet Jason at three.

An hour later, Rina skirted a number of laborers as she made her way across the living room. The varying odors of wax, paint and oils wafted throughout the house as preparations were made to ready Whitney Hall for the upcoming ball. Teams of landscapers combed the many acres, pruning and grooming trees, shrubs, flower beds, orchards and gardens.

The ball was still weeks away, but Abigail directed that refurbishing begin earlier than usual because there were cracks to be spackled and painted, windows to be trimmed and washed, and this year Whitney Hall would wear a new coat of gleaming white paint.

She left the house, slipped behind the wheel of her car and within minutes the powerful surge of the Corvette's engine purred quietly as it ate up the road.

Rina sipped an icy concoction of tropical fruit juices with light and dark rum as she sat waiting for Jason. The exotic drink mirrored her surroundings.

The dark wood-paneled walls, massive potted palms and climate-controlled air made the Palm Garden a popular Savannah meeting and dining spot—all year round.

Securing a table facing a bank of windows, she watched as patrons lingered over late lunch and others arrived for early supper.

She sat forward on her chair when she saw Jason enter the restaurant. As the maitre d' escorted him to her table, she looked past Jason's neatly barbered hair, trimmed moustache and custom-tailored tan suit, and for the first time in more than three years she saw the real Jason Harper. What she saw she did not like.

Jason was unaware of the stiffness in her body as he leaned over to kiss her cheek. "I've missed you, baby."

Rina laid a hand on his arm, pushing him away. "Jason."

A wide grin revealed a set of gleaming porcelain-white teeth. "I know. You hate it when I call you baby."

She motioned to the other chair at the small round table. "Sit down," she ordered.

His smile faded. This was a Rina Jason Harper was unfamiliar with, a Rina Matthews he had never seen before.

He sat down, his practiced smile back in place, while his clear brown eyes moved slowly over her hair and face. She was simply dressed, her hair pulled back in a twist, yet she was flawlessly beautiful.

"I never realized you were so beautiful, Rina. So perfect. It's only now that I realized how blessed I've been."

"How's that?" Her flat tone matched her expressionless face.

"We're the perfect pair. We complement one another."

"You make it sound as if we're prototypes for black Ken and Barbie dolls."

"Why not, Rina? You and me, baby. We're going to make it big. Especially now that you've ingratiated yourself with Cleveland Whitney, and I've managed to land Garritson."

She forced her lips to part in a frozen smile. Jason had given her an opening. "How's Tiffany Garritson, Jason?"

He was prevented from answering when a waiter approached their table. "I'll have what she has," he said nervously, gesturing at Rina's drink.

"That's the house special—a kamikaze, sir," the waiter informed Jason.

Oh, how appropriate, Rina thought, taking a delicate sip of her drink.

She waited until the waiter walked away, saying, "Tiffany Garritson, Jason."

"What about Tiffany Garritson, Rina?"

"You tell me. How is she?" she asked softly. Jason shrugged his shoulders, affecting an air of indifference.

"I suppose she's all right."

Rina leaned forward, her eyes flashing with annoyance. Did Jason really believe she was that naive, or a fool?

"Just all right? The florist delivered more than six hundred dollars worth of plants and flowers to the lady in less than a month. And you have the audacity to sit here and tell me she's all right."

A shadow of rage swept across Jason's handsome face, "Let's get something straight, Rina. Now!" His voice rose slightly, and heads turned in their direction.

She did not see a man's dark eyes watching her from the other side of the room, nor could she sense the tension in the man's large body.

"Yes," she snapped, her voice low and angry. "Let's get it all out in the open. Are you sleeping with Tiffany?" she asked directly. Jason stiffened as if she had struck him, and Rina had her answer.

Opening her handbag, she withdrew a folded sheet of newspaper and threw it at his chest. "You and Tiffany made the social section of last week's paper."

Jason's hands shook slightly as he unfolded the page. He stared down at the images of Tiffany Garritson and himself in a passionate embrace at the party on the Garritson estate.

"That must have been some party," she sneered.

Jason flung the paper to the table. "It was business."

Rina closed her eyes, clenching her teeth. "Don't insult my intelligence." Reopening her eyes, she glared at him. "I know Tiffany is not the first woman you've slept with since we've been together. It's only that now I've chosen not to ignore it."

Jason muttered an expletive under his breath. "Those women meant nothing to me," he explained glibly.

Rina was more shaken than she cared to admit. Somehow she did not expect Jason to openly confess his infidelity. She thought perhaps he would attempt to deny it.

"Why, Jason?"

He reached for her hands, but she pulled them out of his reach. "Why, Rina? Because you were always so unapproachable. There were times when you turned me on, made me so hot that I thought I was going to explode…and…and then you would just put up that damned 'don't touch me' shield. And when you did that I had to have someone else. Any woman."

"You're a liar, Jason. Why didn't you tell me that you wanted me?"

He managed a winning smile. "I guess way back in my head I wanted to save you for marriage."

Rina's smile was cynical and sinister. "It's too bad you didn't save Miss Tiffany, because I'm history, Jason Harper."

She stood up, holding her glass. Jason never had time to react when she walked to his side and emptied the glass in his lap.

She replaced the glass on the table, smiling. "That should cool you down for awhile, baby."

Rina adjusted her shoulder bag and walked out of the restaurant, ignoring the admiring glances that swept over her flattering white silk sheath dress and navy and white spectator sling-strap pumps.

Jason sat stunned as he stared down at the darkening stain on his crisp tan slacks. The waiter brought his drink and he glared up at him.

"Bring me another," he snapped. He had to buy time, because he had no way of knowing how long it would take before his slacks dried enough for him to make a hasty retreat from the restaurant without someone noticing the stain.

The waiter walked away moments before another figure stood over his table. A large hand patted Jason's shoulder and he looked up at a grinning Cleveland Whitney.

"Nice suit, my man," Cleve whispered. He turned, not seeing deep color suffuse Jason's copper-tinged skin. He hoped to catch up with Rina before she left Savannah.

Rina half-walked and half-ran to the parking lot. A small cry of fear escaped her when strong fingers circled her upper arm.

"Can I get a lift back with you, sweetheart?" She nearly fainted in relief.

"What are you doing here, Cleve?" Her voice was low and breathless, as if she had run a grueling race.

"I just finished a meeting at the Palm Garden, and I saw you leave suddenly."

Her eyes widened. "You saw?"

Folding his arms over his chest, Cleve nodded. "I saw."

She lowered her head and stared down at the toes of his highly polished shoes.

"I like your style, Rina." Her head came up quickly.

"As long as I'm not on the receiving end of your temper," he added, smiling.

Cleve took the keys from her hand and opened the door to her car. "I'll drive back." He settled her in the low-slung sports car, handed her his suit jacket, then slipped in beside her.

"Where's your car?" she asked, folding his jacket over her knees.

"At Whitney Hall. I drove up with Mother."

Rina leaned back against the leather seat, closing her eyes. It was over. Her personal relationship with Jason was finally over. And after the November election her business association with him would also end.

Cleve took the highway leading southward, taking furtive glances at her profile. His tension was fever-pitched, threatening to erupt at any moment.

"Sweetheart?"

"Yes, Cleve." Rina smiled, not bothering to open her eyes.

"Are you still going to marry Harper?"

"No, sweetheart," she crooned.

Cleve drummed his fingers on the steering wheel, humming a nameless tune. His smile was wide and dazzling, competing with the brilliant rays of the hot Georgia sun.

"It still doesn't mean that I'm going to marry you, Cleveland Graham Whitney," she stated, opening her eyes and taking in his wide grin,

Not until you tell me that you love me, she thought.

"You'll change your mind, Rina," he shot back confidently. "I'm going to make certain of that," he promised.

Cleve made the trip Lack to Whitney Hall in half the time it would've taken Rina, and she was more than surprised when he passed the house, driving in the direction of the beach.

She hardly had time to collect her thoughts as he skidded to an abrupt halt, gathered her from the car and carried her into his house, taking the stairs two at a time.

Within minutes she lay on his bed, naked. Moments later his clothes lay beside hers in a crumbled heap on the floor.

He came into her outstretched arms like a starving man. It had been a more than a week since they had last made love. Surveying her nakedness, Cleve shook his head.

"You're more than I had ever expected," he whispered in awe.

Rina barely heard him as she visually examined his beautifully proportioned male form. Her hand went to his chest, touching, caressing and committing to memory the feel of flesh, muscle and bone.

"You're so beautiful, Cleveland."

His fingers trailed along her cheek and down to her mouth. His mouth replaced his fingers, and he tasted every inch of her body. He didn't just love her, he worshipped her, and her response to him was wild, unrestrained.

He cradled her face, transfixed by her ardor. A finger searched her tender folds and she closed her eyes, letting out her breath slowly.

"Look at me, darling." She obeyed, her lids fluttering open, "That's it," he crooned. "I want you to see how much I love you and how much pleasure you bring me, Rina."

She registered his declaration of love, but it was soon forgotten as passion swept her up in a maelstrom of ecstasy as he entered her with a strong, smooth thrust of raw possession.

She noted the moisture on his upper lip, the taut skin over his prominent cheekbones and the flaring of his nostrils. She also felt his hardness become harder and larger as his own passions spiraled.

"Rina. Sweet heaven," he gasped against her mouth. Shifting slightly, Cleve withdrew and settled her legs over his shoulders.

Rina stared up at his face and shivered. Desire darkened his face and his eyes. If possible, his eyes were blacker as they bore into her, fusing and permitting her to see what he had never shown or given another woman—his unconditional, unselfish love.

He pulled back, the powerful, pulsing length of him sliding and pushing. Each time he withdrew it was a little more, but each time he thrust it was stronger and deeper.

Rina closed her eyes, giving in to the vortex of sensations as she gripped him. It continued, reaching higher and soaring until she cried out in her awesome climax. Cleve exploded simultaneously, taking her with him in his flight to heaven.

He let her legs slide down, but he did not withdraw from her. They lay joined as one, sated, her head resting on his shoulder.

"Cleveland?" she mumbled drowsily.

"Yes, darling."

"I think I've changed my mind."

"About what?"

"About marrying you."

Cleve shifted, leaning on an elbow. "So you liked that position? It's one of my favorites because I can get in real deep and…"

Rina pulled the pillow out from under his shoulder and hit him with it. "Keep it up, Cleveland Whitney, and I'll change my mind again," she threatened.

He sobered immediately, his eyes shining with moisture. "Thank you, Rina, for having me. You'll never regret it."

She kissed him gently on the lips. "And I'll make certain you'll never regret asking me."

CHAPTER 18

Rina sat at the dressing table in her bedroom applying a coat of deep rose lip color. Emily-Jane sat on the bed, coloring in the book Rina had bought for her.

"Look, Rina. I made a princess who looks just like you do."

She swiveled on the stool and smiled at the childish coloring. "She's beautiful, Emily-Jane." Rina turned back to the mirror, putting the finishing touches on her makeup.

Emily-Jane was dressed for bed. Children were permitted to attend the ball when they reached sixteen, and Emily-Jane had another twelve years before she would put in her first appearance.

There was a light knock on the door. "Come in," Rina called out.

Her eyes widened in surprise as the door swung open and Cleve walked into the room. She was expecting Maddie to come for Emily-Jane.

Turning slowly on the stool, she surveyed his tall figure, resplendent in a double-breasted white dinner jacket. A starched white dress shirt with a wing collar, white bow tie, black onyx studs and cuff buttons, black cummerbund, black dress trousers and patent leather slippers tied his heart-stopping formal attire together.

His gaze moved with agonizing slowness over her feathered, sun-streaked hair, bare suntanned shoulders and arms, and the soft swell of breasts rising above the revealing décolleté of her gown. Rina rose gracefully and yards and yards of black silk chiffon flowed out from her tiny waist

Cleve sucked in his breath, then let it out slowly. "That's quite a dress." He smiled when she dipped low in a fluid curtsy.

"She's a princess, Uncle Cleve," Emily-Jane said in a matter-of-fact tone.

"That she is," Cleve concurred. He moved over to Rina, helping her rise. "You're beautiful, exquisite."

"Thank you," she acknowledged softly.

He smiled and attractive lines crinkled his eyes. "As your fiancé and date for this evening I'd like you to wear something for me."

Cleve reached into the breast pocket of his jacket and withdrew a flat box. Rina knew it contained a piece of jewelry. He had already given her an engagement ring, but she had decided not to wear it until after the election.

He handed her the box, and she opened it after two unsuccessful attempts. She stared numbly at an opera-length, double strand of perfectly matched pearls with a brilliant starburst diamond clasp and a pair of pierced earrings, each with a perfect large pearl suspended from a magnificent star.

"Put them on me, please," she said breathlessly.

Cleve's fingers were hot against her bare flesh as he fastened the pearls around her neck, and Rina savored his gentle touch as he removed the pearl studs from her lobes, inserting the diamond stars.

"You were created for precious jewels, Rina. In your ears, around your neck and on your fingers." He adjusted the pink-hued baubles as they spilled wantonly over her golden-brown breasts.

"Are you a prince tonight, Uncle Cleve?" Emily-Jane asked, breaking the magical spell.

"Yes, I am, Em-Jay," he replied, staring at Rina.

"That means when you marry Rina you'll be a king and she'll be a queen," the child squealed in delight.

"And we'll live happily ever after," Rina said, laughing.

Maddie swept into Rina's bedroom, a radiant vision in white organdy. She stared at Rina, her mouth gaping in surprise. "Oh mercy! Aren't you stunning."

"That she is," Cleve agreed.

Maddie smiled at Cleve. "Well, well, well. Just look at you, big brother. You decided to come out of that stuffy old tuxedo. I like you much better in the dinner jacket."

He bowed slightly from the waist.

"I'm glad you approve, dear sister."

Maddie motioned to Emily-Jane. "Come on, precious. It's time for you to go to bed."

Emily-Jane stuck out her lower lip. "Do I have to, Mama?"

Maddie rested her hands on her hips. "Yes, you do."

Emily-Jane replaced the crayons in a box and gathered her book. "Can I stay upstairs and watch with the big kids, Mama? I promise go to bed when the music comes."

Maddie stared at her daughter, then nodded. "Okay, baby. But only until the music begins."

As they had done more than a hundred years before, Whitney children not yet old enough to attend the ball watched from the third floor landing. Many of the older ones later retreated to the fourth floor cupola and practiced dancing with one another for future balls.

Maddie blew a kiss to Cleve and Rina. "I'll see you two downstairs in five minutes."

Cleve's gaze followed Rina as she brushed out her blown-out hair. It had been trimmed to frame her face, falling to her shoulders in a sensual feathered shag. Whenever she turned her head, the light from the lamp caught the fiery brilliance of the diamonds in her ears. She was a vision of midnight sky with stars. Stars on her dress, stars in her ears, a star around her neck and stars in her eyes.

He held out his hand and she floated toward him, placing her smaller hand in his. His eyes made passionate love to her, caressing her face.

"Are you ready, darling?"

Rina pressed intimately to his side. "Yes, Cleve. I'm ready." And she was; with Cleveland Whitney she was ready for anything.

Her right hand rested atop his left as they slowly descended the staircase. Cleve silently acknowledged the young Whitneys lining the third floor landing, while Rina registered the eerie silence and the curious stares of the people assembled in the expansive living and dining rooms.

She smiled at Barbara and Peter Brandt as she passed them. Peter, with a golden ponytail flowing down his back, winked at her.

Cleve directed Rina to where Abigail, Carole and Maddie stood facing Philip, Darren and Rubel in the center of the living room.

The many lights from the massive overhead chandeliers shone like multifaceted jewels, their glow reflecting off the precious gems circling throats, wrists and fingers.

Abigail had explained that Rina was expected to participate in the age-old tradition of leading the first dance with Noah Whitney's direct descendants. As Cleve's prospective bride, she would be included in this family tradition.

Rina felt as if she had stepped back in time as she took her place beside Maddie. Cleve, as the Whitney heir, took his position opposite Abigail.

Rina glanced at the male Whitneys in their formal finery. Even Darren had shed his expression of somnambulance and smiled affectionately at an ebullient Maddie.

Rubel, facing Rina, gave her a silent wolf whistle. She smiled, winking at a younger physical replica of Cleveland Whitney. Observing twenty-eight-year-old Rubel, Rina knew how Cleve had looked ten years before; however, she preferred the older, more mature version.

The band struck a chord, then began the three-quarter tempo of a quadrille. Cleve stepped forward, bowed to Abigail, then moved past her, stopping in front of Rina. A loud gasp rose from those assembled as they watched him break tradition.

Smoothly, as if it had been rehearsed, Philip moved into Cleve's position, while Rubel shifted and stood opposite Carole, leaving Darren facing Maddie.

Rina's lashes shadowed her gold-green gaze from Cleve's as he swung her into a close embrace. He smiled down at the added color darkening her cheeks. His tight arm tightened around her waist as the sweeping skirt of her gown swirled around the length of his black dress trousers.

"Did you plan this?" she asked, glancing up at him for the first time.

"No," he whispered in her hair. "I realized I couldn't begin this ball without you in my arms."

Her gaze swept over the jet black hair brushed off his high intelligent forehead, then down to his firm mouth. "You broke a tradition," she accused him quietly.

Cleve pulled her closer to his body. "It's only one of many traditions we'll probably break, sweetheart."

Rina nodded, smiling, knowing they would create their own traditions, traditions that would be passed down through succeeding generations, traditions that would be broken by many more arrogant Whitney men and women.

Philip danced with Abigail, Carole with Rubel and Maddie with Darren, and soon everyone joined them for the first dance of the black and white ball for that season.

EPILOGUE

Rina and Cleve lay on the thick rug, staring up at the reflection of leaping flames on the walls, contentedly listening to the arias from Handel's "Messiah" without talking. When the final "Amen' ended, they sighed in unison.

"It's been a wonderful Christmas, Cleve."

He nodded in agreement. "Especially since the good folks of Savannah and the city council have permitted their mayor a week's vacation."

Rina moved closer to him. "It's been a time of firsts. Your first year as mayor and our first anniversary."

"And don't forget your thirty-first birthday, sweetheart," he teased.

She grimaced. "Don't remind me."

"Why not, darling?" He laced his fingers through hers. "You're aging beautifully."

"Speak for yourself, old man."

"Forty isn't old," Cleve said defensively.

"To someone who's sixteen it is," she retorted. Leaning over his prone body, Rina kissed her husband's smooth jaw. "Thank you for your generous gift." He had given her a set of keys to a new sports car.

Cleve shrugged broad shoulders. "You're welcome. I can never think of two gifts for you, for your birthday and Christmas, so one generous one will have to do."

She reached into the pocket of her green and black taffeta skirt, withdrawing a small envelope. "I thought this gift should be given to you in private." All of the Whitneys had exchanged gifts earlier that afternoon.

Her teasing smile filled Cleve with anticipation. Sitting up, he took the envelope and slid a finger under the flap, extracting a printed card. He read and reread the card several times, digesting the words and staring down at the tiny lengths of blue and pink ribbon threaded though the square of vellum.

Rina was inviting him to witness the birth of their son or daughter in early summer. The expected date of delivery coincided with her arrival at Whitney Hall almost two years ago to the day.

"I hope you're pleased, Cleveland," she said, giving him a shy smile.

Cleve's expression registered more than pleasure. The shock and wonder of becoming a father lit up his dark eyes.

"It's the most precious gift I have ever received. Thank you, Rina. Thank you very much." He coughed, clearing his throat.

A smug smile softened her mouth. "You're quite welcome, but I couldn't have done it without your help."

Cleve ran a hand over his hair. "How about that? How about that?" he repeated again and again.

Rina moved over, sitting on his lap, arms curved around his neck. "I wonder what my father and Evelyn will say when we tell them they're going to be grandparents."

"I'm willing to bet Gabriel will be handing out cigars as soon as he hears the news, bragging about how his baby girl is going to make him a grandfather," Cleve teased.

"I'm willing to bet that Evelyn cries," she countered.

Cleve smiled, nodding. "You've got a bet, darling."

Her smile matched his. "Merry Christmas, darling."

He kissed her deeply. "Merry Christmas and happy birthday, love." Holding his wife, he felt love and peace. A very gentle peace.

"I love you, Rina," he stated simply. "I'll never get tired of telling you that."

Rina closed her eyes, her head on his shoulder. "And don't think I'll ever tire of hearing you say it."

And she wouldn't.

2009 Reprint Mass Market Titles

January

I'm Gonna Make You Love Me
Gwyneth Bolton
ISBN-13: 978-1-58571-291-5
ISBN-10: 1-58571-291-4
$6.99

Shades of Desire
Monica White
ISBN-13: 978-1-58571-292-2
ISBN-10: 1-58571-292-2
$6.99

February

A Love of Her Own
Cheris Hodges
ISBN-13: 978-1-58571-293-9
ISBN-10: 1-58571-293-0
$6.99

Color of Trouble
Dyanne Davis
ISBN-13: 978-1-58571-294-6
ISBN-10: 1-58571-9
$6.99

March

Twist of Fate
Beverly Clark
ISBN-13: 978-1-58571-295-3
ISBN-10: 1-58571-295-7
$6.99

Chances
Pamela Leigh Starr
ISBN-13: 978-1-58571-296-0
ISBN-10: 1-58571-296-5
$6.99

April

Sinful Intentions
Crystal Rhodes
ISBN-13: 978-1-585712-297-7
ISBN-10: 1-58571-297-3
$6.99

Rock Star
Roslyn Hardy Holcomb
ISBN-13: 978-1-58571-298-4
$6.99

May

Path of Fire
T.T. Henderson
ISBN-13: 978-1-58571-343-1
ISBN-10: 1-58571-343-0
$6.99

Caught Up in the Rapture
Lisa Riley
ISBN-13: 978-1-58571-344-8
ISBN-10: 1-58571-344-9
$6.99

June

Reckless Surrender
Rochelle Alers
ISBN-13: 978-1-58571-345-5
ISBN-10: 1-58571-345-7
$6.99

No Ordinary Love
Angela Weaver
ISBN-13: 978-1-58571-346-2
ISBN-10: 1-58571-346-5
$6.99

2009 Reprint Mass Market Titles (continued)

July

Intentional Mistakes
Michele Sudler
ISBN-13: 978-1-58571-347-9
ISBN-10: 1-58571-347-3
$6.99

It's In His Kiss
Reon Carter
ISBN-13: 978-1-58571-348-6
ISBN-10: 1-58571-348-1
$6.99

August

Unfinished Love Affair
Barbara Keaton
ISBN-13: 978-1-58571-349-3
ISBN-10: 1-58571-349-X
$6.99

A Perfect Place to Pray
I.L Goodwin
ISBN-13: 978-1-58571-299-1
ISBN-10: 1-58571-299-X
$6.99

September

Love in High Gear
Charlotte Roy
ISBN-13: 978-1-58571-355-4
ISBN-10: 1-58571-355-4
$6.99

Ebony Eyes
Kei Swanson
ISBN-13: 978-1-58571-356-1
ISBN-10: 1-58571-356-2
$6.99

October

Midnight Clear, Part I
Leslie Esdale/Carmen Green
ISBN-13: 978-1-58571-357-8
ISBN-10: 1-58571-357-0
$6.99

Midnight Clear, Part II
Gwynne Forster/Monica
   Jackson
ISBN-13: 978-1-58571-358-5
ISBN-10: 1-58571-358-9
$6.99

November

Midnight Peril
Vicki Andrews
ISBN-13: 978-1-58571-359-2
ISBN-10: 1-58571-359-7
$6.99

One Day At A Time
Bella McFarland
ISBN-13: 978-1-58571-360-8
ISBN-10: 1-58571-360-0
$6.99

December

Just An Affair
Eugenia O'Neal
ISBN-13: 978-1-58571-361-5
ISBN-10: 1-58571-361-9
$6.99

Shades of Brown
Denise Becker
ISBN-13: 978-1-58571-362-2
ISBN-10: 1-58571-362-7
$6.99

2009 New Mass Market Titles

January

Singing A Song...
Crystal Rhodes
ISBN-13: 978-1-58571-283-0
$6.99

Look Both Ways
Joan Early
ISBN-13: 978-1-58571-284-7
$6.99

February

Six O'Clock
Katrina Spencer
ISBN-13: 978-1-58571-285-4
$6.99

Red Sky
Renee Alexis
ISBN-13: 978-1-58571-286-1
$6.99

March

Anything But Love
Celya Bowers
ISBN-13: 978-1-58571-287-8
$6.99

Tempting Faith
Crystal Hubbard
ISBN-13: 978-1-58571-288-5
$6.99

April

If I Were Your Woman
La Connie Taylor-Jones
ISBN-13: 978-1-58571-289-2
$6.99

Best Of Luck Elsewhere
Trisha Haddad
ISBN-13: 978-1-58571-290-8
$6.99

May

All I'll Ever Need
Mildred Riley
ISBN-13: 978-1-58571-335-6
$6.99

A Place Like Home
Alicia Wiggins
ISBN-13: 978-1-58571-336-3
$6.99

June

Best Foot Forward
Michele Sudler
ISBN-13: 978-1-58571-337-0
$6.99

It's In the Rhythm
Sammie Ward
ISBN-13: 978-1-58571-338-7
$6.99

2009 New Mass Market Titles (continued)

July

Checks and Balances
Elaine Sims
ISBN-13: 978-1-58571-339-4
$6.99

Save Me
Africa Fine
ISBN-13: 978-1-58571-340-0
$6.99

August

When Lightening Strikes
Michele Cameron
ISBN-13: 978-1-58571-369-1
$6.99

Blindsided
Tammy Williams
ISBN-13: 978-1-58571-342-4
$6.99

September

2 Good
Celya Bowers
ISBN-13: 978-1-58571-350-9
$6.99

Waiting for Mr. Darcy
Chamein Canton
ISBN-13: 978-1-58571-351-6
$6.99

October

Fireflies
Joan Early
ISBN-13: 978-1-58571-352-3
$6.99

Frost On My Window
Angela Weaver
ISBN-13: 978-1-58571-353-0
$6.99

November

Waiting in the Shadows
Michele Sudler
ISBN-13: 978-1-58571-364-6
$6.99

Fixin' Tyrone
Keith Walker
ISBN-13: 978-1-58571-365-3
$6.99

December

Dream Keeper
Gail McFarland
ISBN-13: 978-1-58571-366-0
$6.99

Another Memory
Pamela Ridley
ISBN-13: 978-1-58571-367-7
$6.99

Other Genesis Press, Inc. Titles

Other Genesis Press, Inc. Titles (continued)

Other Genesis Press, Inc. Titles (continued)

Everything but Love	Natalie Dunbar	$8.95
Falling	Natalie Dunbar	$9.95
Fate	Pamela Leigh Starr	$8.95
Finding Isabella	A.J. Garrotto	$8.95
Forbidden Quest	Dar Tomlinson	$10.95
Forever Love	Wanda Y. Thomas	$8.95
From the Ashes	Kathleen Suzanne	$8.95
	Jeanne Sumerix	
Gentle Yearning	Rochelle Alers	$10.95
Glory of Love	Sinclair LeBeau	$10.95
Go Gentle into that	Malcom Boyd	$12.95
Good Night		
Goldengroove	Mary Beth Craft	$16.95
Groove, Bang, and Jive	Steve Cannon	$8.99
Hand in Glove	Andrea Jackson	$9.95
Hard to Love	Kimberley White	$9.95
Hart & Soul	Angie Daniels	$8.95
Heart of the Phoenix	A.C. Arthur	$9.95
Heartbeat	Stephanie Bedwell-Grime	$8.95
Hearts Remember	M. Loui Quezada	$8.95
Hidden Memories	Robin Allen	$10.95
Higher Ground	Leah Latimer	$19.95
Hitler, the War, and the Pope	Ronald Rychiak	$26.95
How to Write a Romance	Kathryn Falk	$18.95
I Married a Reclining Chair	Lisa M. Fuhs	$8.95
I'll Be Your Shelter	Giselle Carmichael	$8.95
I'll Paint a Sun	A.J. Garrotto	$9.95
Icie	Pamela Leigh Starr	$8.95
Illusions	Pamela Leigh Starr	$8.95
Indigo After Dark Vol. I	Nia Dixon/Angelique	$10.95
Indigo After Dark Vol. II	Dolores Bundy/	$10.95
	Cole Riley	
Indigo After Dark Vol. III	Montana Blue/	$10.95
	Coco Morena	
Indigo After Dark Vol. IV	Cassandra Colt/	$14.95
Indigo After Dark Vol. V	Delilah Dawson	$14.95
Indiscretions	Donna Hill	$8.95
Intentional Mistakes	Michele Sudler	$9.95
Interlude	Donna Hill	$8.95

Other Genesis Press, Inc. Titles (continued)

Intimate Intentions	Angie Daniels	$8.95
It's Not Over Yet	J.J. Michael	$9.95
Jolie's Surrender	Edwina Martin-Arnold	$8.95
Kiss or Keep	Debra Phillips	$8.95
Lace	Giselle Carmichael	$9.95
Lady Preacher	K.T. Richey	$6.99
Last Train to Memphis	Elsa Cook	$12.95
Lasting Valor	Ken Olsen	$24.95
Let Us Prey	Hunter Lundy	$25.95
Lies Too Long	Pamela Ridley	$13.95
Life Is Never As It Seems	J.J. Michael	$12.95
Lighter Shade of Brown	Vicki Andrews	$8.95
Looking for Lily	Africa Fine	$6.99
Love Always	Mildred E. Riley	$10.95
Love Doesn't Come Easy	Charlyne Dickerson	$8.95
Love Unveiled	Gloria Greene	$10.95
Love's Deception	Charlene Berry	$10.95
Love's Destiny	M. Loui Quezada	$8.95
Love's Secrets	Yolanda McVey	$6.99
Mae's Promise	Melody Walcott	$8.95
Magnolia Sunset	Giselle Carmichael	$8.95
Many Shades of Gray	Dyanne Davis	$6.99
Matters of Life and Death	Lesego Malepe, Ph.D.	$15.95
Meant to Be	Jeanne Sumerix	$8.95
Midnight Clear	Leslie Esdaile	$10.95
(Anthology)	Gwynne Forster	
	Carmen Green	
	Monica Jackson	
Midnight Magic	Gwynne Forster	$8.95
Midnight Peril	Vicki Andrews	$10.95
Misconceptions	Pamela Leigh Starr	$9.95
Moments of Clarity	Michele Cameron	$6.99
Montgomery's Children	Richard Perry	$14.95
Mr Fix-It	Crystal Hubbard	$6.99
My Buffalo Soldier	Barbara B. K. Reeves	$8.95
Naked Soul	Gwynne Forster	$8.95
Never Say Never	Michele Cameron	$6.99
Next to Last Chance	Louisa Dixon	$24.95
No Apologies	Seressia Glass	$8.95

Other Genesis Press, Inc. Titles (continued)

Other Genesis Press, Inc. Titles (continued)

Other Genesis Press, Inc. Titles (continued)

Order Form

Mail to: Genesis Press, Inc.
P.O. Box 101
Columbus, MS 39703

Name _____
Address _____
City/State _____ Zip _____
Telephone _____

Ship to (if different from above)
Name _____
Address _____
City/State _____ Zip _____
Telephone _____

Credit Card Information
Credit Card # _____ ☐ Visa   ☐ Mastercard
Expiration Date (mm/yy) _____ ☐ AmEx ☐ Discover

Qty.	Author	Title	Price	Total

Use this order form, or call 1-888-INDIGO-1	Total for books _____
	Shipping and handling:
	$5 first two books,
	$1 each additional book _____
	Total S & H _____
	Total amount enclosed _____
	Mississippi residents add 7% sales tax